The Alien Interviews

Little Gray Aliens Spill Their Secrets

Chet Novicki

Table of Contents

PART 1 - BACKSTORY
Chapter 1 – Dead Jimmy

Many years ago, when I was a young man and a member of the U.S. Army, I was a student at the Army Language School in Monterey, California. I spent a year there, studying Chinese Mandarin. The school is still there, high on the hill overlooking the city and Monterey Bay, only now it's called the Defense Language Institute Foreign Language Center. A classier, more modern-sounding name, I guess.

Jimmy Chisholm was the best student in our class. Languages came easy to Jimmy. He spoke Spanish and Portuguese before he came to the school, and he picked up Mandarin with ease. His accent and tone control were considered near-perfect by our teachers.

And then one day, about six months into the course, Jimmy disappeared. He didn't show up for class. His roommate hadn't seen him for days. No one knew what had happened to him.

Rumors began to swirl around the Mandarin department, and eventually spread to other language departments, as well. All of them were ridiculous. Jimmy had defected to China. No, Jimmy had run away to Mexico with a girl he met in Salinas. No, that wasn't it, either – and this one was my favorite – Jimmy had been kidnapped by little green men and taken aboard a flying saucer.

Eventually, the rumors became so much of a distraction that the Army sent a big shot officer to talk with us about what had happened to Jimmy. According to this officer – I think he was a colonel but I don't remember his name – our classmate had been involved in a head-on car crash on the narrow, treacherous, winding road out to Big Sur, and had perished at the scene.

Almost before we had time to digest this disturbing piece of news, we were confronted with an even greater shock. Jimmy's parents had arrived from Atlanta to pick up his body and take it back to Georgia for burial. But before they left, they wanted to meet Jimmy's classmates and friends. Our entire class was ordered to meet with them and to comfort them as best we could.

Jimmy's father was stoic – no tears or showing of emotion. He thanked us for meeting with him and seemed to appreciate our sharing of stories about our interactions with his son. But his mother was the complete opposite, constantly crying and insisting on talking to each of us individually. Of course, we each tried to console her and tell her nice things about her recently-deceased son – an only child, I might add.

And that was that. The shock was short-lived. Jimmy's parents left and went back to Atlanta by train, taking his body with them. My Chinese class resumed. And life went on. I finished my year-long course in Mandarin, got sent overseas and spent a couple of years in various Asian locales. Eventually I came back to the states, got out of the Army and resumed civilian life. I got married, had a couple of kids, then got divorced. And I pretty much forgot about Jimmy.

Until one day, forty years later, as I was sitting around thinking about my fast-approaching retirement, I received a phone call. From Jimmy. Yeah. *That* Jimmy. The dead guy.

"I know you must think it's strange," he said, after he told me who he was. "Me calling you after all these years, I mean. I realize we never were really close friends."

"What I think is strange is that I'm talking to a dead man. Jimmy Chisolm died years ago."

"Yeah. I know. Car crash in Big Sur. In the fog."

"Exactly. So, who are you and what are you up to?"

"Did you ever see the body?"

"What?"

"My body. Did you ever see it? Or my car? The one I was supposedly driving 50 miles an hour on that twisting Big Sur road. In the fog."

"No. But I met your parents. Or Jimmy's parent, I should say."

"Actors. Both my parents died when I was nine. I was raised by my aunt and uncle."

"What?"

"Not my parents. Professional actors. Hired to portray my parents."

"Hired? Who hired them?"

"The government."

"Why?"

"To make it look like I was really dead."

I'm not sure if this is when I started to believe that the guy on the other end of the line was really Jimmy Chisolm, or if it was just curiosity about where this was heading, but I said, "All right. So, say I believe you. Why would the government want people to think you were dead?"

"It was an excuse to pull me out of class and assign me to a special, super-secret project without me having to explain to anyone what was happening."

"Super secret, huh?"

"Yes. It was. They trained me to talk to aliens. EBEs."

I don't know what I was expecting Jimmy – if it really was Jimmy – to say, but that wasn't it. "Aliens?" I said.

"Well, not talk to them, exactly. They don't talk. They communicate telepathically."

"Of course they do."

"No, really. I spent over 20 years communicating with them. Grays. The little ones."

"Listen, if this is a joke, it's gone far enough. Just because I'm a science fiction writer – "

"It's not a joke. And that's exactly why I'm contacting you."

"Because I write science fiction?"

"Because you're a writer. And this is that kind of story."

"Science fiction, you mean?"

"No. Not fiction. This is real. But it's about aliens."

"Uh-huh."

"I know this is hard to believe," he said.

"Boy, that's an understatement."

"I'm pretty sure I can convince you I'm Jimmy Chisholm."

"Okay. Go ahead."

"Well, I was in class the day you got the tones mixed up on the word *bi* and told Mrs. Yang you wanted to use her pussy, when you were supposed to say you wanted to use her pencil. And Mrs. Yang slapped you."

Oh. An embarrassment from my past, something I'd *almost* completely forgotten. "Lots of people knew about that," I said. Which was true. Word of my slip of the tongue and Mrs. Yang's reaction had spread quickly throughout the Mandarin Department, and then beyond.

"Yeah, I guess so. Okay. One time you, me, and a guy from another class – Craig, I think his name was – went to Mephisto's for pizza. The old place. The one they tore down for urban renewal. There was this waitress there you had the hots for. Laurie something. Have to admit, she was pretty sweet. But she was about six years older than you and had a kid, and you weren't even old enough to order a beer with your pizza."

Holy crap! This guy really was Jimmy Chisholm, back from the dead. How else would he have known about Mephisto's and my long-ago crush, the beautiful Laurie?

"Okay. So maybe you are Jimmy," I said. "What do you want from me?"

"Nothing. I want to send you something."

"What? Your book?"

"No. There is no book. Just 20 years of notes – *detailed* notes – about every conversation I ever had with the aliens."

"And you want to send them to me?"

"Yes."

"Why? Do you want me to turn your notes into a book for you? Something like that? I don't really do stuff like that."

"That would be nice, I suppose. But I don't really care what you do with them. I just need to tell someone."

"I don't get it," I said.

"Look, I've been sworn to secrecy my entire life. Unable to tell anyone what I know, unable to tell anyone how I spent my life, all the secrets I know. I know the answers to many of mankind's greatest questions, but I've never been able to tell anybody. Do you know how frustrating that is?"

I didn't, but I could imagine. "So now you're going to talk?"

"Yes."

"By telling me your story?"

"Yes, that's right."

"Why don't you just write a book and self-publish it? It's easy to do, these days."

"I don't have time."

"Oh, sure you do. A couple of hundred words a day and you'll have a book in less than a year."

"I don't have a year. The doctors say three months. Maybe four. That's why I'm doing this now."

"Oh, ... I'm sorry to hear that."

"It's okay. I've come to grips with the whole dying thing. Since I've done it before, you know."

I really didn't know how to respond to that.

"So, can I send you my notes? You can do whatever you want with them – write a book, throw them away, whatever you want. Just promise me you'll read them."

"All right. Send them to me. I promise I'll read them."

"Great. Just one more thing."

"What's that?"

"All I have is your phone number and an email address. I need your physical address."

I gave him my address and hung up, wondering ... well, wondering about lots of things, actually. Mostly, wondering about where all this would lead.

Chapter 2 – The Package

A box from Jimmy arrived five days later by Priority Mail. It was tucked behind my kitchen steps, where it couldn't be seen from the street, when I got home from grocery shopping. That's where Bitsy, my regular letter carrier, usually leaves packages for me. Apparently, the intent is to discourage porch pirates, although I haven't heard of that really being a problem around here.

As soon as I picked up the box, a sudden flash of doubt hit me. About what I'd agreed to do, I mean. Jimmy had described what he wanted to send to me as *notes*, but the box weighed at least 10 pounds – probably more. That was a *lot* of notes. I hoped they were as exciting and revealing as he'd claimed they were.

Once in the kitchen, I placed the box on the kitchen table, out of the way, and set about putting away my groceries. Usually, I only shop about every two weeks. The Publix Supermarket I shop at is about 15 miles away, and I buy a lot of heat-and-serve frozen items like turkey dinners and pizzas. Oh, and chocolate ice cream – I *love* chocolate ice cream. So getting those items into my freezer, once I get home, is always a priority. Otherwise, I'm sure I would have made opening the box my number one concern, as my curiosity about the notes had grown exponentially in the days waiting for Jimmy's package to arrive.

After I had the groceries put away, I turned my attention to the box. Jimmy – or whoever had packed it – had wrapped it with so much packing tape it was impossible to open. Frustrated, I grabbed a paring knife from my counter and cut off one end of the box.

As the contents spilled out onto my kitchen table, I immediately saw why the box had been so heavy. Inside were three loose-leaf binders. But these weren't regular binders – not the kind you might have used in high school or college. These suckers were *huge*! Each was about two inches thick and contained hundreds of pages. And on the outside of each binder was a neatly-printed plastic label identifying the contents –

Interviews with Alien #1, *Interviews with Alien #2*, and *Interviews with Alien #3*.

A cold beer in one hand and the binder labeled *Alien #1* in the other, I went into the living room and settled into my recliner to see what Jimmy had to say. Excitement and nervousness fought for control of my emotions as I stared at the binder cover. What would I find inside? Would it be revolutionary information that would change mankind's understanding of alien beings and our place in the universe? Or perhaps just the fantasies of a wacked-out, seriously-disturbed person?

After all, I hadn't seen or heard from Jimmy in over 40 years. That's usually the way it works with dead people – you don't see them or hear much from them. What if Jimmy wasn't, as he claimed, an alien interviewer? What if he was just a good old-fashioned nut job?

Or, what if Jimmy – the Jimmy on the phone and the Jimmy who sent me the box – wasn't Jimmy, at all, but someone perpetrating a prank, or some kind of scam? Although, try as I might, I couldn't think of anyone who would go to as much trouble as this entailed. For a brief moment, I pondered the possibilities the binder might contain a live snake or might explode when I opened it. I'm not sure if I'd call that normal caution or paranoia.

Eventually, though, I opened the binder. My excitement and nervousness were immediately replaced by disappointment – the first page was entirely in code. So were the second and third. I flipped quickly through the binder – the pages weren't numbered but there were hundreds of them – looking for the key to the code but couldn't find it. Nothing but page after page of what looked like a simple substitution code filled the binder.

Searching through the pages of binders #2 and #3 yielded identical results. Everything was in code, and there was no key. *Thanks a lot, Jimmy!* What was I supposed to do with this? Maybe this whole thing *was* a prank of some kind.

I got another beer from the fridge and leaned back to consider my predicament. The obvious thing to do was to give Jimmy a call and find out what was going on. So that's what I did – I got my phone, scrolled down my log to when I'd gotten the call from Jimmy, and ... the entry was gone. There was no call from Jimmy.

Thinking I'd gotten the day wrong, I checked the log for the two days before and the two days after. Nothing. I checked three days in each direction, then five. Still nothing. According to my phone, I'd never received a call from Jimmy.

Hmm. Very strange. I decided to go check the box in which the binders had been shipped. And that's when I found it, wrapped in a small piece of bubble wrap and taped to the inside of the box. A flash drive.

Finally, I thought. The key. But when I plugged the flash drive into my computer's USB port, it didn't contain the key to the code. The only documents on the drive looked to be copies of the material in the binders – interviews with the three aliens, in code.

It appeared I'd hit a dead end. Unsure of what my next step should be, I returned to the living room, finished my beer, turned off the light, leaned back in my recliner, and promptly fell asleep. I've always felt that, in uncertain times, a short nap can be of tremendous help in clearing up confusion and helping to set a course of action. And that was my hope this time – that I'd nod off and wake up in a half hour or so with a plan, some idea of what to do next.

I must have been pretty tired. Almost three hours later I awoke, groggy, with the taste of stale beer heavy in my mouth. The house was dark, the living room illuminated only by a dim glow coming from outside and the bright blue numbers of the clock across the room, which proclaimed it was 9:42. I struggled to my feet and started for the bathroom, intending to brush my teeth and pee, not necessarily in that order.

That's when I noticed that, although the house was dark inside, the faint glow coming from outside was coming from my outside lights. My motion-activated floodlights were on. I wondered if that was what woke me, but at the same time I had the feeling I'd been awakened by a noise, not by the lights.

A quick glance out my living room window revealed an empty front lawn. I thought perhaps a neighbor's dog had wandered onto my property and triggered the lights – that's happened before. More than once, in fact. But I saw nothing unusual out on my lawn, only long, fuzzy shadows cast by the floodlights.

I left the interior lights off and went into the kitchen. The window above the sink offered a wider view of the yard and surrounding area than did the window in the living room – easily visible were the front of my garage, the driveway, and the street that fronted my house. I cracked open the blinds and peeked out.

The yard was empty. But, just as I turned away and headed for the bathroom, a car door slammed, out on the street. I looked out the window again. Down the street, about a half-block away, a car was parked, barely visible beneath a broken street lamp. And, as I watched, the car pulled out and vanished down the street into the darkness.

Nothing odd about that. There are houses all up and down this street, and people come and go at all hours of the day and night. Except for one thing. When this car pulled out and disappeared into the night, the driver never turned on his headlights.

Hmm.

Chapter 3 – Teresa

In retrospect, calling my friend, Teresa, and telling her about Jimmy and the notebooks was a mistake. This was a story I should have kept to myself. I shouldn't have involved her.

But I did.

My friendship with Teresa began a few years ago during one of my grocery runs to Publix, in Bartow. The store was relatively empty of customers and I was just getting started, cruising up and down the aisles, not paying much attention to where I was going, mostly just checking out the nearly endless array of available snacks and goodies. I'm a big fan of snacks and goodies.

As I turned into the 'cookies' aisle, my cart ran head on into the cart of a very attractive Hispanic woman who was doing the same as me. Not paying attention to where she was going, I mean. We took turns apologizing.

"I'm so sorry," I told her.

"No, no. It's my fault. I wasn't looking where I was going." She smiled, obviously embarrassed.

"Well, that makes two of us. And I am sorry," I said.

"Don't be. I'm sure I'll survive." She smiled again – nice, straight, white teeth set into a well-tanned, friendly face, maybe 40 years old, with medium-long, black hair just starting to show a few streaks of gray. I think the word *cute* would be a good way to describe her.

I nodded and started to leave, but she stopped me.

"Don't I know you?" she said.

I looked back at her. She didn't look familiar. "I don't know. Do you?"

"I think maybe I do. Can you take off your cap? And your sunglasses? So I can see you better."

I removed my shades and cap and smoothed out that gray stuff on the top of my head, trying to make myself look presentable. "How's this?"

"You sure look familiar, but I can't place you. Are you famous or something?"

I laughed. "Far from it. *Really* far."

"What do you do?"

"I'm a writer. I write – "

"Science fiction! You're Chet Novicki!" she blurted out. "I knew I recognized you."

I'm pretty sure my jaw must have dropped open when she said that. While it's true I'm a science fiction writer and have written a few books, I'm not famous and never have been, and *no* stranger has ever recognized me in public before. "I don't believe it," I said.

"What? That you're Chet Novicki, the famous writer?" She giggled.

"No. That you recognized me."

"I'm your biggest fan. I have all the Podok books, even the box set. And some of your songs, too. I have *The Fudgecats* album."

"You're kidding!"

"It's true."

A large woman, her cart pile high with frozen pizzas, beer, and a variety of chips, rounded the corner. Finding her way blocked by our carts, she gifted us with an "ahem," followed quickly by a "harrumph!" We moved to one side and let her pass.

"This is all very hard to believe," I said.

"I know. Do you live here? Or are you just visiting?"

"Here. Well, in Fort Meade, actually."

"I live here, in Bartow. I can't believe you live around here. And that I met you."

At this point, I think I blushed and said something lame – "Yeah, it's a small world," or something to that effect.

We chatted on for several minutes. She obviously had read my books – she described the plots of a couple of them in detail. And she told me about herself. Her name was Teresa, she was 41, single, and she was an office assistant for a local dermatologist. She was also, in her words, "the world's biggest science fiction fan."

Eventually, though, it was time to continue our shopping. We said our goodbyes and I thanked her for recognizing me. Ego wise, I was feeling pretty good as I walked away, heading for the frozen food section.

Five minutes later, Teresa and I bumped into each other again – figuratively, this time – in the ice cream section.

"Stocking up?" I said, eyeing the two containers of ice cream in her cart.

"Yeah. It's Buy One Get One Free on Edy's ice cream. That's my favorite."

"Guess I'll get some, then. I like it, too."

"You know, I was thinking … " she said.

"Uh-huh?"

"Can we stay in touch?"

"What?"

"Stay in touch. Like, maybe … by email?"

"Well, … "

"I promise I won't harass you, or anything like that."

And that's how our friendship started, with an exchange of email addresses. Over the course of a few months we progressed from emails to phone calls, and then to dating and a hot romance that eventually flamed out, but left us where we are today. Friends. Really good friends.

So, Teresa being a good friend, I regret involving her in all this. But I did, and there's nothing I can do about it. And, of course, I didn't know then what I know now.

* * * * *

"What!" said the self-described 'world's biggest science fiction fan' when I called her the following morning and told her about Jimmy and the notebooks. "What! You're kidding me!"

"Nope. It's true. He died 40 years ago. Or, at least, I thought he did."

"But, obviously, that wasn't so."

"I guess not."

"And? What did they say? The notebooks."

"Well, I looked at them, but I couldn't read them. They're written in some sort of code."

"What kind of code?" she said.

"I don't know. It's just long lines of letters of the alphabet. No spaces, like between words – just letters. And each page has two or three paragraphs of these lines, each paragraph separated by a couple of skipped lines."

"So, do you have – what do they call it? The key?"

"Yeah, the key. And no, I don't have it. The only things in the box were the three notebooks and the flash drive."

"That's kind of strange. That he'd send you stuff in code but not include the key."

I agreed with her assessment of the situation. It *was* strange.

"Maybe it's not that difficult," she suggested.

"What's not difficult?"

"The code. Maybe it's just a simple substitution code. Where you move letters one or two spaces to the left or the right. Have you tried that?"

"No. Besides, what's the point? If the code's that easy to break, why bother to encode it?"

"Yeah, I guess you're right. Why bother?"

"Anyway, I know absolutely nothing about codes."

There was a long pause on Teresa's end.

"You still there?" I said.

"Yeah. I was thinking."

"Oh, oh."

I could almost hear her grinning at my comment as she said, "I could ask my Uncle Bill. He was in the Army."

"So?"

"He was in the Army Security Agency."

"Hey, so was I. That's how I went to language school and studied Chinese. The ASA sent me."

"He worked with codes."

"Oh. Well, then, that sounds like a great idea," I said. "Tell you what. I've gotta go shopping later this afternoon. I'll swing by your place and drop off a copy of the flash drive for you to show to your uncle. Sound good?"

"After five. I won't be home until around five."

"All right. I'll see you then."

"I can hardly wait to see this stuff," she said, and hung up.

*****

It was almost six when I got to Teresa's. She popped the flash drive into her laptop and we spent almost an hour looking at the copies of the notebooks, eventually agreeing that none of it made any sense at all. We'd probably still be there, trying to figure out the code, but I had to go back to Publix and pick up a couple of items I'd forgotten the day before, so I left the flash drive with Teresa, to show to her uncle, and left.

A couple of days went by without much happening. My yard stayed dark at night and there were no strange cars out on the street. I know because I checked. So I wrote off my previous suspicions as paranoia and tried to resume my normal life.

The notebooks still sat on my living room floor, in front of my recliner, where I'd stacked them for easy access. Six or seven times a day – probably more – I'd pick one up and thumb through it, although I don't know why. I couldn't read any of it. Maybe I thought if I stared at the code long enough, I'd get an inkling of how it worked. Or that the long lines of nonsensical letters would somehow magically rearrange themselves into something that made sense. But they never did.

With magical intervention apparently out of the question, Teresa's Uncle Bill seemed to be our last hope of breaking the code. He lived down south, in Tequesta, about 150 miles away, but Teresa had made plans to meet up with him over the coming weekend, to visit with family and to give him a copy of the encoded notebooks. So I was more than a little surprised when Teresa called me at five past seven on Friday morning, waking me up.

"What's happening?" I mumbled into my phone.

"Did I wake you?"

"No, I was just getting up," I lied.

"Guess what I'm doing?"

"I don't know. Talking to me on the phone? What?"

"I'm sitting in my car, outside my house."

"How come? Car trouble? You need some help?"

"No. Not car trouble. It's just ... there's about a hundred cops in my house, and it was so crowded I kept getting in the way, so I came out here."

"Police? A hundred of them?"

"Well, maybe more like six. Or eight. But my house is small – you know that."

"Why are the police in your house?"

"I was robbed."

"Robbed?" I sat up in bed, suddenly wide awake.

"Yeah. Or burgled. Is that a real word? Maybe burglarized – that's it. Someone broke into my house."

"Were you home? Are you okay?"

"Yeah, yeah, I'm fine. A little shaken up, but okay. I woke up and they were in my bedroom. I think there were three of them. I screamed when I saw them and one of them – this really big guy – flipped me over and stuck a needle in my butt, and that put me back to sleep."

"You're kidding!"

"No, I'm not. So when I woke up a little while ago, I called the police. And now they're searching through my house, looking for clues."

"So ... what? Did they steal a bunch of your stuff?"

"No, that's one of the funny things about all this. All they took was my computer. Where I'd copied your notebooks."

"That's it? Just your computer?"

"Yeah."

"That's okay. I've still got the notebooks," I said. "I can make more copies."

"That's good."

"What else?

"Else?"

"Yeah. You said taking your computer was *one* of the funny things about all this. What else was funny?"

"Oh, yeah. But you're not going to believe this part."

"Maybe I will. Try me."

"One of them – the burglars, I mean – was an alien. A little gray, outer-space alien!"

Chapter 4 – Aliens?

Teresa was right. That last part was a little hard to believe. "What!" I said. "Say that again."

"One of them was a little gray alien."

"Are you sure this wasn't a dream?" I said.

"Well, I've got a big lump on my butt where they stuck me with the hypodermic needle and my computer's missing. I didn't dream that."

"Yeah, I guess not. What did the cops say when you told them about the alien?"

"I didn't tell them."

"No?"

"No. I didn't want to sound like a wacko. So I left out the part about the alien, and – hang on a second, one of the cops is motioning to me."

I waited. I could hear Teresa talking to someone – presumably the cop – but I couldn't quite hear what he was saying. After a short while, Teresa resumed our conversation.

"I'm back," she said. "I've gotta go. The cops want to talk to me."

"Okay."

"Listen, if you're not busy, why don't you come up here? I don't really want to get into this on the phone, but there's more to this story."

"Yeah?"

"Yeah. A lot more."

"Okay. I'll be there in an hour or so. I assume you're not going to work today."

"You assume right," she said, and hung up.

I washed up and got dressed, then piled into my old Buick LaCrosse and headed for Bartow. On my way out of town I stopped at McDonald's and bought two large coffees. By the time I got to Bartow, some 20 minutes away, they'd be almost cool enough to drink.

No cops or cop cars were in sight when I arrived at Teresa's. I parked in her driveway and, coffees in hand, went inside. She was seated at her kitchen table, filling out an official-looking sheet of paper.

"I brought you a present," I said, taking a seat opposite her and sliding one of the coffees across the table.

"Thanks."

"The cops left?"

"Yeah. They gave me this form to fill out – it's called a Victims' Impact Statement – and they went back to the station to file a report. They said don't hold my breath waiting to get my stuff back."

I nodded, agreeing with the official assessment of the situation. "I've heard people seldom get their stolen items back."

"So, how much do you think my old laptop was worth?" she said.

"I don't know. How old was it?"

"I'm not sure. Four, maybe five years. So, ... ?"

"Three hundred dollars, maybe? Computers are cheap these days."

"This one wasn't cheap. Not when I bought it, anyway." She turned her attention back to her paperwork. "Estimated value of items – one thousand, eight hundred dollars," she said, writing the numbers down as she spoke.

"Really?" I said. "You're going to claim it was worth that much?"

"Sure." She smiled. "It's just an estimate. I don't even remember what I paid for it. And I don't understand computers, of course, 'cause I'm a girl and we girls just can't handle complicated things like computers. Everyone knows that." She stuck her tongue out at me in a playful manner.

I laughed and took a sip of my coffee. Still hot.

"Anyway," she continued, "I'm not trying to make a buck, here. I just want to make sure this thing goes down as a felony. Maybe that way they'll actually investigate it. If I claim my computer was only worth a couple of hundred dollars, it'll be just another misdemeanor among thousands, and they'll never get to it."

"I guess you're right."

"I'm pretty sure I am." She signed and dated the bottom of the paper and took a sip of her coffee.

"So, tell me what happened," I said. "You said there was an alien?"

"Yeah. It was so weird. This big guy – the guy who flipped me over and poked me with the needle – was sitting on top of me. On my shoulders, facing my feet. His butt was pressing down on the back of my head, pushing my face into the pillow. I thought I was going to suffocate. I could feel myself, like, slipping away, getting dizzy and with darkness rushing in from each side. And the drug they gave me was making my brain feel all fuzzy."

"That sounds pretty scary."

"It was. I thought I was dying. I thought that guy was going to sit on my back until I was dead."

"But you're okay, now. Right? No post traumatic stress or anything?"

"No. I was upset when I woke up and realized what had happened, but now I'm just kinda pissed off."

I chuckled. Teresa's a mellow person – she gets excited sometimes but she seldom shows anger.

"It's not really funny, you know." She took another sip of her coffee, then continued, "But – and this is the weird part – just before I was about to pass out, that big guy got off me and then he turned my head to one side so I could breathe."

"So he was ... what? Just waiting for you to conk out? Not trying to kill you?"

"Maybe. That's what I thought, at first."

"But then?"

"Well, when he turned my face to one side, he turned it toward the room. That's when I saw the alien."

"The little gray you mentioned."

"Yes. It was strange, though. If he'd turned my face in the other direction, the only thing I would have seen was my wall. But he turned it toward the room. It's like he wanted me to see that alien."

"Why?"

"I have a theory," she said.

"I'm sure you do." I wasn't surprised. Teresa always had lots of theories. About lots of different things. Why should this be any different? "What is it?" I said.

"When he was sitting on me, he wasn't trying to kill me, he was waiting for me to get nice and sleepy – just waiting for that drug to go to work – before he let me see the alien."

"*Let you* see the alien?"

"Yeah. That's my theory. That they wanted me to see the alien, just before I nodded off, while I was all groggy and foggy and everything."

"Why? Why would he want you to see the alien?"

"Good question. I don't know. Maybe so no one will believe me when I tell them how it happened. The burglary, I mean. That's why I didn't tell the police. I didn't want them to think I was a nut, some kind of crank or something."

"Seems like a lot of trouble. Two humans and an alien to break in and steal a computer? Sounds like a one-person job, to me."

"Yeah, maybe. But I didn't tell you the best part."

"And that would be?"

"I think the alien was fake. It wasn't a real little gray."

"Really? Why?"

"Well, it *looked* like a gray. It was short and it had that V-shaped head and the big black eyes, but it was too husky. Real grays have skinny little bodies and long, spindly arms and legs. Right?"

"Yeah, I guess so. I've never seen a real one, but that's the way they're portrayed in the movies."

"This one was stocky, with short arms and legs. And – here's the kicker – it had a beer belly."

"What?"

"A beer belly." She made a motion with her hands that looked as if she was describing a pregnant woman. "A big one, too."

"That's not right," I said. "Little grays do not have beer bellies."

"Exactly."

"So, they not only stole your computer, but they put on a show of doing it, and they made sure you saw it. And, just for good measure, they threw in a fake alien. Why go to all that trouble, I wonder?"

"Yeah, why? And *who*?"

Chapter 5 – Premonitions

Teresa offered to make breakfast for us but I declined. Instead, we went into town, to Perkins, a family restaurant where you can get breakfast anytime they're open. It was while I was chowing down on a ham and cheese omelet that I began to get an uneasy feeling. Not from the food – that was fine. It was more like a … a premonition, a feeling something bad was about to happen. I closed my eyes and a vision of me in a terrible automobile accident appeared. I shook my head and chased it away.

"Something wrong?" Teresa wanted to know.

"No. I'm fine. Just trying to clear my head of all this confusing info."

"I know how you feel," she said.

After we ate, I dropped off Teresa at her place and headed home. The feeling of dread stayed with me, but I couldn't put my finger on exactly what it was about. Was I getting a psychic warning about an impending accident? Just to be on the safe side, I obeyed all the speed limits and stayed in the right-hand lane all the way back to Fort Meade. It was only when I got into town and had to turn left that I moved over into the left lane. No sense taking any chances, I figured.

As I started to pull into my driveway, though, I realized my interpretation of my 'uneasy feeling' had been completely wrong. It wasn't about me getting into a traffic accident. Apparently, it had been intended to warn me that someone was breaking into my house, because my kitchen door was open, swinging back and forth in the afternoon breeze. I was pretty sure I'd locked it when I left for Bartow.

I parked and cautiously approached the door. For all I knew, the intruder – or intruders – was still in the house. Holding the door open, I carefully stuck my head around the open doorway. No one was in my kitchen, which was likely a good thing. If there had been, I probably would have been shot dead, right in the middle of my forehead.

I listened carefully for noises from other parts of the house but didn't hear any. After waiting for a couple of minutes to build up my courage, I finally went inside and searched the house until I was satisfied that whoever had broken in was now gone.

Not only was the intruder gone, so were the three notebooks and my computer. After a quick look around, I determined nothing else was missing, just the notebooks and my laptop. It was pretty clear now what they were after, both here and at Teresa's – the notebooks. But who *they* were, and why they wanted them, was a little more difficult to comprehend. Was it some government agency, trying to keep us from finding out the secrets hidden in that code? Because they were classified documents, maybe? Or did the notebooks contain valuable information – information that might be worth a fortune and would justify a couple of thefts and putting on a little show with a fake alien? It also occurred to me that, no matter why they wanted them, there was also the question of how they even knew the notebooks existed.

I suppose I should have called the police and reported the break-in, but I didn't. For one thing, Fort Meade doesn't have police. Although incorporated as a city, it's really just a small town in the country. There's hardly any crime, and the town had decided a few years ago that cops were a luxury they couldn't afford and didn't need. So, no police station, no police cars, and no policemen. There was a sheriff's sub-station in town, but I'd never had any dealings with them and I didn't know if they investigated these kinds of crimes. I'd always thought of sheriffs as being more involved with traffic enforcement than investigating crimes.

So many questions. I decided to call Teresa and let her know what had happened. But as I pulled out my phone to make the call, I realized that at least one obvious way someone could have found out about the notebooks was to have been listening to Jimmy's original call to me. Although I doubted anyone had been listening into *my* phone conversations, someone might have been listening to Jimmy's. Especially if that someone worked for the government. And, once

Jimmy called me, they – whoever *they* were – might have started listening into my phone conversations, too.

I called Teresa, anyway. Not to talk about what had happened, but to let her know I was coming back up to see her. She didn't answer, though. The call went to voicemail. Almost immediately, that uneasy feeling – that vague premonition I'd had when we were eating at Perkins – returned. And, along with the uneasiness, a new, disquieting thought wriggled its way into my consciousness. In the excitement of the story about the fake alien and my subsequent discovery of the missing notebooks at my place, I had completely overlooked an important part of all this – the flash drive I'd given to Teresa. When we'd talked, earlier, neither of us had even mentioned it. Of course, I still had my laptop and the notebooks then, and the existence of the flash drive wasn't that important. But now, with both of our computers and the notebooks gone, that flash drive was the only copy of the notebooks we still had. That is, if she still had it.

I really needed to talk to Teresa again. Also, I was a little worried that she hadn't answered her phone – that wasn't like her. I got back in my car and made excellent time all the way back up to Bartow, arriving at her house in 16 minutes. A new record.

My second 'premonition' of the day turned out to have been a false alarm, however. Teresa was fine, as I found out after pounding loudly on her kitchen door for a minute. She'd been taking a nap when I called. Evidently, the drug the burglars had given her had produced a delayed, hangover-like effect, and she'd been trying to sleep it off.

"You're back?" she said, all messy-haired and sleepy-eyed.

"Yeah. We need to talk."

"Okay. Let me go wash my face," she said, letting me in. And then, as she was heading for the bathroom, she mumbled, "I thought we already talked. Was that a dream?"

"They stole my notebooks!" I yelled after her, but she'd already closed the bathroom door and I guess she didn't hear me. I sat down at the kitchen table and waited for her to return.

"Okay. What's the problem?" she said when she came back, taking a seat across from me.

"While I was up here with you, earlier, someone broke into my place and stole my computer and the notebooks."

"You're kidding! Just like me."

"Exactly." I told her the story of my arrival home to find my kitchen door swinging in the breeze.

"And you think it's the same guys who broke in here?" she said when I'd finished.

"Well, I didn't see them, but it makes sense, doesn't it?"

"Yeah, it does."

"So, here's my question. What happened to the flash drive I gave you? Do you still have it?"

"Oh! The flash drive – I forgot all about it. No, I don't have it. It was in the computer they stole. It was still in the USB port."

"Crap!"

"But I made a copy."

"What?"

"I made a copy of the flash drive. I got to thinking about what you told me, about how the call from Jimmy disappeared from your phone log, and how the lights came on in your yard and the car with no headlights, and a little voice told me it would be a good idea to make a copy. So I did."

"That's great. What did you do with it?"

"I hid it."

"Where?"

"In the garage."

"So let's go get it," I said.

Chapter 6 – Danny

"It's over there, in the corner. With those tools," Teresa said, as she turned on the lights in the dim garage and pointed to the correct corner.

"I don't see any tools," I said.

"Uh, they should be right there." She looked from corner to corner of the empty garage, but there were no tools. "Damn! They took the tools, too. They were right there. In that corner."

"Well, they're not there, now," I said, stating the obvious.

"Yeah. It's kind of weird, though. There were a bunch of these plastic containers, with nails and screws and other little thingies in them – fasteners of some kind, I think. And I hid the flash drive in one of the containers."

"What's weird about that?"

"How did they know? I didn't tell anyone about the tools. Or about hiding the flash drive with them. I didn't even mention it to you."

"You could have told them when you were stoned on that drug, " I suggested.

"I doubt it. If I told them, they'd know the drive was in a container. They wouldn't have to take all the tools. There was a power saw, a nail gun, lots of tools. And they took them all."

"Maybe it wasn't them. Maybe Danny took them. They were his tools, weren't they?" Danny was Teresa's ex-husband, a carpenter. A frequently unemployed carpenter.

Her face brightened. "Danny! Of course. That's it – the burglars didn't take the tools, Danny did. He still has keys to the place. He could have picked them up when I wasn't home."

"That's great, then. That means – "

"That he's got the flash drive," she said, finishing my sentence.

"Easy to find out for sure. Give him a call."

We went back into the house and Teresa called Danny. Or rather, she tried to call him. Without success, though, as she hung up without saying anything.

"What? He's not there?" I said.

"I got a message – phone not in service. What's that mean?"

I shrugged. "I dunno. That he's not near a cell phone tower, maybe?"

"Yeah, maybe. But there are cell towers everywhere. It would be hard to get out of range of one."

"Maybe he's on a boat, out in the middle of the gulf somewhere. Or in the Atlantic. Repairing dolphin habitats or something."

Teresa laughed. "I doubt that. Danny *never* goes near the ocean. Not since he saw the movie *Jaws*."

"Actually, me, either. Not since *Jaws*."

She laughed again. "What a couple of wusses," she said.

"I think of it as being smart. Me and Danny. Two smart guys."

"So I wonder why his phone's not in service, then."

"Maybe he got a new one. With a new number."

"Yeah, maybe. But now we can't get in touch with him."

"Well, we could go see him. He still lives around here, doesn't he?" I said.

"Up in Dade City. He moved up there about two or three months ago."

"You know where?"

"I've got his address. But it's almost two hours away from here – straight up US 98. It takes almost an hour just to get through Lakeland."

"We don't have a choice, though. We need the flash drive – it's the only copy of the books we have and Danny's got it." And then, to be on the safe side, I added, "Most likely." No sense tempting fate.

"Okay, I guess you're right," she said. "So let's do it. "Let's go see him. And let's hope he's home."

"Yeah, let's hope he's home," I agreed.

We took my car. I gassed up in Bartow and we headed north, up route 98. Traffic wasn't too bad as we left Bartow, but as we approached Lakeland, a long, stretched-out city about 15 miles away, the afternoon rush hour was underway and things slowed down considerably. Teresa had been spot-on with her prediction – as we left North Lakeland, heading for Dade City, we'd been stuck in bumper-to-bumper traffic for almost exactly an hour.

"Traffic never gets this bad in Fort Meade," I commented.

"Bartow, either," she replied.

By the time we arrived in Dade City, almost two hours had elapsed since we left Bartow, so Teresa was right about that, too. We spent another 30 minutes searching for Danny's place on Sapphire Valley Road, cruising up and down the hilly terrain. The land up here is a lot hillier than in Bartow and Fort Meade, which are pretty much flat. It's cooler, too.

We finally had to stop and ask for directions, which I've always found a bit embarrassing. A 'real man' should be able to find his way around, without assistance. At least, that's what my father used to say. But I was always lousy at directions and my old Buick didn't have modern luxuries – like GPS – so we were dependent on a paper map, and it wasn't a lot of help. And yeah, while my car may not have had much in the way of modern technologies, it did have two things going for it – it was extremely reliable and the loan was paid off long ago.

So I stopped at a gas station and Teresa went inside to talk to the attendant. Have you ever noticed that gas station employees tend to be much more attentive and friendly to attractive women than they are to men? That's why I wasn't surprised that, when Teresa returned, she commented, "What a nice guy!"

"I'm sure," I said.

"No, really. He was very friendly."

"Did he ask you for a date?"

She punched me in the arm. Not lightly, either. "No, silly. He didn't."

"Then, did he know where Danny's place is?"

"Yeah. Go up three blocks, turn right and then Sapphire Valley Road is the first left."

With the instructions from the gas station attendant, finding Danny's house was easy. Finding Danny, however, was more difficult – he wasn't home. Teresa knocked for two minutes on the front door while I checked in the back yard and the detached garage.

I guess we looked like suspicious characters because, after a couple of minutes, an elderly man came out of the house next door and approached us. "Can I help you folks with something?" he asked as he walked up to us.

"We're looking for Danny," I said.

"You friends of his?"

"I'm his ex-wife," Teresa said.

"Oh. Well, Danny's been gone for a while. Saw him loading up his truck with stuff a couple of days ago, and then he took off and I ain't seen him since."

"Darn," said Teresa. "I tried to call him but his phone's been disconnected or something. We drove all the way up here from Bartow, trying to get in touch with him. I don't suppose you know where he went?"

"Nope. Didn't get a chance to talk to him before he left."

"If you see him, will you ask him to call Teresa. That's me. And tell him it's important."

"Teresa. Sure, I can do that."

We thanked him and I gave him one of my business cards – the ones that say, *Author Chet Novicki* – just to assuage any lingering suspicions he might have had about us.

"You a writer?" he said.

I nodded. "Uh-huh."

"Whaddaya write?"

"Science fiction."

"Oh. Too bad. I like mysteries."

"Yeah. Lots of people do," I said. "Even me."

As added insurance, Teresa left a note stuck in Danny's front door, asking him to call her. Then we thanked the next-door neighbor and drove away, leaving him standing in Danny's driveway, waving goodbye to us. It was starting to get dark as we picked up 98 South back to Bartow, a couple of hours away. It had been a long day. I was disappointed and tired and I wasn't looking forward to the drive home.

We had spent the entire afternoon on our little excursion to Dade City and it appeared to have been a waste of time. Whether or not Danny unknowingly had the flash drive was still a big question mark. And even if he had it, it didn't do us much good if we didn't know where he was. The only thing we had really learned from our trip was bad news – Danny was gone and we didn't know how to contact him.

Chapter 7 – The Note

It was dark when we got back to Bartow. I pulled into Burger King as we went through town and we went inside for a couple of Whoppers and a shared Coke. By the time we got back to Teresa's, it was after 10 o'clock.

"You want a beer?" she yelled from the kitchen as I flopped my tired body onto her overstuffed living room couch.

"Sure," I yelled back.

She came back with a couple of beers, put one on the table in front of me and sat down next to me. "Wanna watch TV?" she said.

"Nah, I'm too tired."

"Good. Me, too."

We sat there, relaxing, drinking our beers and thinking about our situation. At least, that's what I was thinking about – I don't know if Teresa was thinking the same thing as me. But what I was thinking was, without the notebooks or Danny's flash drive copy of them, we were at a dead end.

"We really need to find out what happened to Danny," she said.

So, she *was* thinking the same thing as me. "Yeah. Well, when he comes back and finds your note, I'm sure he'll call you."

"Let's hope that's soon. I'd really like to find out what it says in those notebooks."

"You should hope he still has the flash drive. He could have found it and just thought it was a piece of junk that didn't work anymore and thrown it away."

"Gee, you're a real Mr. Sunshine."

"Or maybe dumped out the jar of nails and lost it."

She stuck out her tongue at me.

"And even if we get the flash drive back, we won't be able to figure out what it says. Everything's in code."

"Well, I guess we should just give up, then," she said in her most cynical voice.

"Maybe we should. I'm beginning to think we're in over our heads, anyway."

"No way," she said. "We can't quit in the middle of a great story like this."

I didn't feel like arguing. "Yeah, maybe. Whatever. We'll see what happens."

It was when Teresa went to get our second beers that she discovered the note. It had slipped down the side of the 12-pack and absorbed a lot of moisture, and it was stuck to one of the bottles when she pulled it out. But, even though it was soaking wet, it was still legible. And, ... it was from Danny.

"Hey, look at this," she said, when she came back in the living room with the beers. "It's a note from Danny."

"What's it say?" I said, sitting up from my semi-reclined and exceedingly-relaxed position on Teresa's couch. Beer tends to do that to me, I've noticed. Encourage me into semi-reclined and relaxed positions, I mean.

"He got a job. Working with some friend of his, doing hurricane reconstruction up in the panhandle. And he took his tools. And he's got a new phone."

"Great."

"Let's call him," she suggested.

I glanced at Teresa's big round wall clock, staring at me from across the room. It was well after 11 o'clock. "It's kinda late," I said.

She checked the clock. "All right. We can call him tomorrow, then."

"Yeah, that sounds better."

"You wanna stay over? I can cook us up some breakfast in the morning and then we can call him."

"Don't you have to go to work?"

"Not really. When I called work to tell them I wasn't coming in because of the break-in and the cops being at my house and everything, my boss told me to take as much time as I needed to recover from the 'trauma.' I figure that's going to take at least a couple of weeks. Besides, this is way more interesting than work."

"I guess. So. Spend the night, huh? That sounds, uh, ... interesting."

She grinned. "In the guest room."

"Darn," I said.

We sat around talking while we finished our beers, then Teresa fixed me up with some fresh towels and a new toothbrush and I got ready for bed. I really wasn't expecting to get a good night's sleep – I'm a restless sleeper and usually don't sleep well in beds other than my own – but this bed was surprisingly soft and snugly and I fell asleep almost immediately. The last thing I remembered was pounding my pillow into a comfortable shape and thinking, *this is a very nice bed.* And then, there was Teresa, waking me for breakfast.

"Hey, lazy bones, you gonna sleep all day?" she said.

I rolled over and rubbed my eyes. "Good morning to you, too. What time is it?"

"A little past nine. C'mon, get up. Breakfast is almost ready."

I washed up and attempted to comb that patch of gray stuff on top of my head. Once that was a nice, healthy jungle of brown hair but, of course, that was long ago. Now it was just an erratic mess of gray crabgrass that resisted all efforts to make it look presentable. I smoothed a few spots into place with my hand, sighed at my aging reflection in the mirror, and joined Teresa in the kitchen.

"What are we having?" I said, as I slid into a chair at the kitchen table.

"Yakimeshi," she said, placing a mug of coffee on the table in front of me. Hot and black, just the way I like it.

"What the heck is that?"

"It's like, uh ... breakfast fried rice."

"Really?"

"Yeah, really. It's delicious. It's got eggs and onions and ham and, of course, rice. My neighbor, Natsuko, taught me how to make it."

Teresa's assessment of yakimeshi's flavor was completely accurate – it was, as she'd described it, 'delicious.' She served it with toast and jam, and I wolfed everything down with the enthusiasm of a man who usually survives on fast food, TV dinners and frozen pizza. "That was great," I said when were finished eating.

"Obviously," she said, smiling. "You eat just like a pig, you know."

"You should take that as a compliment. Your cooking is so-o-o-o good!"

We took our coffees into the living room and settled onto the couch.

"So, call Danny?" I said.

"I guess so." She pulled out her phone and the note, which had dried out overnight. "What should I say?"

"Whaddaya mean? Just ask him if he has the flash drive."

"Yeah, but Danny's the curious type. He's gonna ask questions."

"About what?"

"About everything. What's on the flash drive, how come I hid it in a jar of nails, stuff like that."

"Oh. Well, then ..."

"What? I can't tell him the truth, can I?"

"I don't know. What is the truth? What is it that we're doing?"

She looked thoughtful. "I think we're investigating a conspiracy – a government conspiracy, most likely – involving aliens. Outer space aliens."

"You probably shouldn't tell him that," I said.

"I didn't think so. Then what *should* I tell him?"

I probed my brain, searching for some logical reason Teresa would hide a flash drive in a container of her ex-husbands nails. Finally, I said, "He knows about me, right?"

"Uh-huh, he knows we're friends. And that we dated for a while."

"He knows I'm a writer, doesn't he?"

"Yeah, he does."

"All right. Tell him we're writing a book together. And the flash drive is a backup copy of notes for the book, and you hid it there – with the nails – just in case."

"Just in case what?"

"I don't know. Your computer crashed, your house got robbed, whatever."

"He's going to have a hard time believing I'm writing a book. I never wrote anything in my life – I'm a reader, not a writer."

"So tell him you're helping me with research for my new book."

"Okay, that sounds better. What's it about?"

I resisted the urge to say, "about three hundred pages," and instead said, "You know, aliens and secret government bases on the moon – something like that."

"Really?" she said. "That's what you want me to tell him?"

"Sure. Why not? I *am* a science fiction writer, after all."

"Yeah, I guess so." She picked up her phone and punched in Danny's new phone number. "It's ringing," she said.

"Always a good sign," I said. "Put it on speaker so I can hear the conversation."

Chapter 8 – The Call

Danny's new phone rang for an inordinately long time before anyone answered. And the person answering the phone was not Danny – he introduced himself as, "Investigator Tellis Mims, Bay County C.I.D." Obviously, this was not what Teresa had been expecting, and it rattled her. Just a bit.

"Uh, ... um, ... I, uh ... guess I have the wrong number," she said.

"Ma'am?"

"Sorry." She hung up.

"That went well," I said.

"Yeah. Did I get the number wrong?" She picked up the note and compared it to the phone number on her log. "No. This is right," she said, answering her own question.

The phone rang, startling her and causing her to jump back slightly. She looked at it. "It's the number I just called. Danny's number."

"Answer it."

"Hello," she said. "Danny?"

"No, ma'am. This is Investigator Mims. I believe we were speaking, just a short while ago?"

"Oh. Yes. But I was trying to call Danny Richardson and I got you by mistake. I'm sorry. I didn't mean to bother you."

"It's not a problem, ma'am. This is Mr. Richardson's phone. Might I inquire as to your name?"

Teresa glanced over at me with a funny look on her face. A *what-the-heck-is-going-on?* kind of look. "It's Teresa," she said. "Teresa Ruiz."

"Are you a friend of Mr. Richardson's, Teresa?"

"Yeah, sort of. He's my ex-husband."

"I see. Well, I'm sorry to be the bearer of bad news, but, ..." Investigator Mims' voice faded away.

"But what?"

"Well, this isn't the kind of news I'd normally deliver over the phone."

"I'm hundreds of miles away. Down in Polk County. How else are you going to deliver it to me?"

"Right. Well, Teresa, I'm sorry to tell you this, but your ex-husband has been the victim of a violent crime."

"A violent crime?" Teresa's forehead crinkled into a worried look.

"Yes, ma'am," said Investigator Mims. And then, "Perhaps you should sit down while I tell you about this."

"I *am* sitting down."

"All right, then. I'm here at your ex-husband's place in Mexico Beach. It's a trailer he was living in while he was doing some carpentry work, fixing up places, according to the few neighbors he had. There's not much left here, after the hurricane, you know."

"Neighbors? You've been talking to his neighbors?"

"Yes, ma'am. They sent me down here from Panama Beach after some local folks called us. I'm a homicide investigator."

Teresa had been leaning forward, but when she got this piece of unsettling news, she slumped back against the couch and said, "Homicide? Oh, no!"

"I'm afraid so," said Tellis Mims.

"What happened?"

"We've actually just started our investigation but it appears that Mr. Richardson – your ex-husband – came home and interrupted a burglary in progress. And ... he got shot in the process."

"This is almost impossible to believe," she said. A single tear leaked from her right eye and rolled down her cheek. She wiped it away with her hand.

"I'm sorry for your loss," said Investigator Mims.

"Thank you."

"Would you mind answering a couple of questions for me?"

"I guess not. What kind of questions?"

"Are there others we should notify about this? Next of kin?"

"His parents are still alive. They live down in Arcadia. And he has a sister – Janice – but I don't know where she lives. Georgia, I think. Or maybe it's South Carolina. All this information is probably in his wallet. He carries a little contact card in it."

"His wallet is missing, ma'am. Along with just about everything else."

"Oh ... yeah. Well, maybe it's on his phone, in his contacts list."

"This phone – the one I'm using right now to speak with you – appears to be new. There are no contacts. In fact, your earlier call is the only incoming call in the phone's log."

"That's kinda strange."

"Ma'am?"

"You said just about everything's missing."

"Yes, ma'am."

"But not his phone?"

"No, ma'am. His phone was still here. Actually, we don't know, for sure, that *anything* is missing. But we're assuming this was a break-in, a robbery gone wrong, because there's nothing much here – in his trailer, I mean. And it appears the place has been searched, as if they were looking for something specific."

"I see."

"You wouldn't know what that might be, would you?"

"No, I wouldn't." Teresa gave me a quizzical look. I could almost tell what she was thinking – *was someone looking for the flash drive?*

"Was your ex-husband a drug user?" Investigator Mims wanted to know. "Could someone have been searching for drugs?"

"I don't think so. We're on fairly friendly terms, but we don't exactly hang out together, you know. We've been divorced for almost 10 years. But Danny was never into drugs, back when we were together."

"I understand. Do you have any idea of what someone could have been searching for? Did your ex have personal items of value that might interest a thief?"

"I don't know. Well, he had tools. Lots of them. Carpentry tools. Nail guns and stuff."

"We didn't find any tools."

"Anyway, a thief wouldn't have had to search for his tools. Danny was never very good at putting things away. Most likely they would have been in plain sight – probably right in the middle of the living room."

"I see. Anything else?"

"I can't think of anything."

"May I inquire as to the nature of your call, this morning? Why, exactly, were you attempting to contact your ex-husband?"

"Well ... uh, it has to do with the tools."

"Yes?"

"Did you find any nails? Containers with nails in them? Like, six or seven of these little plastic jars, filled with nails and screws?"

"We did find a container like that. But not six or seven – just one. It was open and someone had dumped the contents out onto the floor. It was mostly nails."

My spirits sank when I heard that. It sounded as if someone had been looking for the flash drive. And found it.

Teresa responded with, "Damn!"

"Ma'am? Is there something significant about that jar of nails?" Investigator Mims said.

"You only found one jar?"

"Yes, ma'am."

"You see, he had these tools stored at my place. In my garage. And he picked them up when I wasn't home. And I'm pretty sure there were several jars of nails and screws with the tools, not just one. And he took everything. There wasn't anything left behind."

"I see. Is there something special about these nails?"

"No. But I hid something in them. In one of the jars."

"And what was that?"

"A flash drive." Teresa squirmed around on the couch and gave me a look that said, *What am I supposed to tell him?*

I responded by ignoring her and taking a sip of my coffee. It was cold. I hate cold coffee. I got up, went into the kitchen and nuked it, standing in the doorway so I could continue listening to the conversation.

"Ma'am?" he said. "Did you say you hid a flash drive in a jar of nails?"

I could practically hear the wheels in Investigator Mims' head spinning as he processed this new information. A flash drive was something associated with espionage – was that what was going on? Had he stumbled onto an international espionage ring? Was this the case that was going to kick his career into high gear? Maybe even get him promoted to captain?

"That's right. I didn't know Danny was going to come get his tools – they'd been sitting in my garage for a while. A pretty long while. So I thought that would be a good place to hide it."

"And why, exactly, would you need to hide a flash drive in a jar of nails?"

Teresa proceeded to tell Investigator Mims the story of how her house had been burglarized and her computer had been stolen – all of which was true, of course. She left out the part about her being home at the time and seeing the fake alien. I guess she thought that would make her story even more unbelievable than it already was. She then embellished the story by claiming she was writing a book and the flash drive contained a copy of her notes. "I figured, if I got robbed again, no one would bother to take a jar of nails, you know. I didn't think Danny would take them when I wasn't home," she told Mims.

"I see," he said. "Well, we've searched the place pretty thoroughly and we didn't find a flash drive."

"That's too bad. I'm not sure what I'll do now."

An awkward pause – at both ends of the conversation – followed. Finally, Teresa said, "Well, if there's nothing else ..."

"I can't think of anything right now. But if I have any more questions, I'll be in touch. Is this a good number to reach you at?"

"Yes. It's my cell phone. Will you let me know what happens?"

"I will. I'll keep you informed. And I'm very sorry for your loss," Investigator Mims said.

"Thank you." She hung up, looked at me and began to cry.

Chapter 9 – Dead End

"I don't believe it. Danny's dead." Teresa stared at her coffee, now cold on the table in front of her. She seemed to be in shock.

"I'm so sorry," I said, realizing, even as I said it, how mundane and inadequate it sounded.

"Murdered."

"Yeah. Strange."

"I never knew anyone who got murdered."

"Me, either."

"Do you think …?"

"What?"

"You know …" she said.

"That there's a connection? To the notebooks and the robberies and stuff?"

"Yeah."

"Maybe. At least, that's what it looks like."

"What are we going to do now? Everything's gone. The notebooks, the flash drive, all of it."

I shrugged. "I don't know. It looks like we've reached the end of the line."

"I can't believe they'd kill him. Just to get the flash drive."

"That probably wasn't part of their plan," I said.

"And how did they even know about it? That I hid it in that jar of nails?"

"Yeah. That's a mystery, for sure."

"I feel terrible," Teresa said. "This is all my fault."

"No, it's not. You can't blame yourself for this. It's not your fault at all."

"Yes, it is. If I hadn't become involved in all this, Danny would still be alive."

"We don't know that. This might have had nothing to do with what happened down here. It could just have been a robbery gone bad."

"I doubt that," she said.

Actually, I doubted it, too. It was almost a certainty that Danny's murder was somehow connected to what had happened to us. The thefts at our houses, down here in Polk County, I mean.

"I'll be back in a little while," Teresa said. She got up and went down the hall into her bedroom, closing the door behind her.

Experience had taught me what was going on – I'd seen this happen before. More than once. This was Teresa's way of handling really bad news. She'd go into her bedroom, shut the door, and have herself a good cry. Then, after 10 minutes or so, she'd come out and tell me she was "feeling better."

And that's almost exactly what happened this time. Ten minutes later she came out of the bedroom, eyes all puffy and red, but instead of saying she was feeling better, she said, "I still can't believe it."

I agreed with her, nodding my head and saying, "Yeah, it's hard to believe."

"We really need to do something about this," she said.

"Like what?"

"I don't know. Like, ... something."

"I don't see that there's much we can do. The notebooks are gone, the flash drives are gone, and we don't even know what they said. What do you want to do? Go to the police and tell them about the little gray alien with the beer belly?"

She made that crinkly-nosed face people sometimes make when a particularly rotten smell surprises them. "No, I don't want to do that."

"What, then?"

"I don't know. I can't really think of anything."

"Well, I've gotta go to Walmart," I said, deliberately changing the subject in an effort to get Teresa to think about something other than Danny.

"What's at Walmart?"

"Computers. I need a new computer. So do you."

"Yeah, I know."

"You wanna go with me?"

"No. I don't feel like shopping. I'm not in the mood."

"I'll buy you lunch," I offered.

"Thanks, but no."

"All right. I think I'm just going to go to Walmart and then go home and try to forget all about this. Jimmy, the notebooks – all of it. Just put it out of my mind. Maybe get back to work. I haven't written anything since I got that call from Jimmy."

"Great," she said, without a lot of enthusiasm.

"You going to be okay?"

"Yeah. It was the shock, you know. Finding out the way we did. I thought I was going to talk to Danny and I ended up talking to that cop, instead. And then he tells me Danny's been murdered."

"You're sure you're okay?"

"I'll be fine. Go ahead and go on home. Or Walmart or wherever."

I put my coffee cup in the kitchen sink and yelled, "Call me if you need to talk," as I went out the kitchen door.

"Think of something to do," she called after me.

Yeah. That's what I needed to do – think of something. But as I climbed into my car and headed over to the Walmart Supercenter, just a few blocks away, I was pretty sure I wouldn't be able to think my way out of this. We really were at a dead end. Barring a miracle, our little adventure had come to a complete stop.

The parking lot was full – it usually is. There really isn't any other place in Bartow to shop for items other than groceries. If you wanted a new TV or a pair of jeans or a fishing pole – anything like that – Walmart was the place to get it. It was either there or a trip up to Lakeland.

I guess I'm what you'd call a *quick shopper*. With the exception of buying groceries, I hate to shop, so I don't spend time looking around, checking out new products or things like that. I'm just in and out in record time. And this little shopping trip was no exception. Less than 15 minutes after arriving, I was back in my car, heading home to Fort Meade with a brand-new, price-reduced, el cheapo brand laptop – all I needed to write my books and do a little online research. And it had only dinged my credit card for $350 plus $24.50 in state and county sales taxes.

It's funny the way things work out, sometimes. All the way back to Fort Meade, I alternated between feelings of depression and anger. The depression came from knowing Teresa and I wouldn't be playing this game anymore. And that's what it had become to me – a game, a mystery to be solved. What did it say in the notebooks, and on the flash drive? And who took them? And why?

And when I wasn't depressed, I was angry. Because now we'd never know how all this would have turned out. We were left hanging, with no resolution to what had become a really interesting story, and I hated that feeling. I wanted to know the ending.

That's what was in my head as I arrived home, parked in my driveway and made my way into the house – a combination of anger and depression. But as I started up the steps into my kitchen, I noticed a package had been slipped into Bitsy's usual delivery spot. Well, not a package, really. One of those white, almost-impossible-to-open, polypropelene envelopes, like the kind Amazon uses.

I picked it up and looked at the address label, and my anger and depression were instantly replaced by feelings of anticipation, hope, and then happiness. The hand-written label appeared to have been written by the same person who sent me the notebooks – dead Jimmy, presumably – and it had been mailed from the same zip code in Chicago. I opened my kitchen door and went inside, a smile on my face. Maybe – just maybe – Teresa and I were back in the game.

Chapter 10 – Turnaround

My joy at finding the envelope was short lived. Inside was a flash drive and a note that said, *Guess you'll be needing this, too. J.* I assumed the *J.* stood for *Jimmy* and that was a good thing. But another flash drive? I had a sneaking suspicion that this flash drive, if it contained what I thought it did, wasn't going to be of much use to me and Teresa.

I spent the next two hours setting up my new computer, using the *Easy Setup Guide* that came with it. The guide was apparently written by someone in a country far, far away who was not particularly well-versed in English grammar. Or English vocabulary, either.

But eventually, notwithstanding the incomprehensible instructions of the guide, I got my new laptop up and running, hooked up to the internet and ready for use. So far, so good. I downloaded and installed a free copy of OpenOffice so I could use their word processor and also to prove to myself that everything was working properly. Satisfied that it was, I popped the flash drive into the USB port, eager to see what Jimmy had sent me.

The elation I'd felt when I first saw the envelope from Jimmy quickly dissipated when I saw what was on the flash drive. My earlier suspicion had been correct. It was the key – the key to the code used to encode the notebooks. Jimmy had either forgotten to include it with his original package or, more likely, had sent it separately as an extra measure of security.

Great. Just what I needed – the key to decode the three notebooks I no longer had. If I hadn't been so disappointed, I'm sure I would have laughed at the irony. And the thought that this was all just a really, *really* elaborate prank also reappeared.

I pushed the prank theory out of my head. This was not a prank. Pranks do not include burglaries, home invasions with a fake alien, and now, a murder. So, if it wasn't a prank, what *was* going on? And who was behind it?

I got a beer from the fridge and settled into my recliner to contemplate the problem. Two beers later, I had the solution – it was the government. No one else could have known about dead Jimmy's phone call, the package with the notebooks, Teresa's involvement, her hiding the flash drive in the jar of nails, and Danny taking them. It had to be the government.

So. It was the government. Now what? Would they be coming after me again, trying to get the flash drive with the key? Did they even know I'd received it? Did they care, now that I didn't have the notebooks?

The thought that another beer might help me clear up this last part of the puzzle occurred to me, but I was sleepy from the beer I'd already consumed and decided a short nap might be more beneficial. You know, one of those 30-minute snoozes where you fall asleep with a question and wake up with the answer. That's always been one of my favorite ways of seeking a solution to a problem.

It was almost six o'clock. I considered setting my alarm clock but it was far away, on the other side of the room, and would have necessitated leaving my comfortable, siesta-inducing recliner. Not a good idea, I decided. Instead, I leaned back in my chair, put my feet up and promptly fell asleep.

I was still asleep when my phone rang at seven-thirty and woke me. It was Teresa, sounding more excited than I'd ever heard her. "I need to see you," she said.

"What's up?" I sat up in my chair.

"Guess what! Guess what happened!"

"What?"

"C'mon, guess. Take a guess."

"I don't know," I said, eyeing my warm beer and wishing it was cold. "You won the lottery?"

"Yeah, that's it. I won the lottery. No, silly. I just went out and checked my mail and guess what I got?"

"Do I have to keep guessing all the way through this story? What did you get?"

"The flash drive!"

"What?"

"The flash drive! Danny sent it to me."

No doubt it was the combination of the beer, the nap, and the sudden awakening clouding my thought processes, but I found this information difficult to comprehend. Wasn't Danny dead? How could he send a flash drive – or anything, for that matter – to Teresa? I shook my head, trying to eliminate the fuzziness that filled it.

"You still there?" Teresa said.

"Yeah, yeah, I'm here. But I'm confused."

"It's simple. Danny found the flash drive I hid in the jar of nails and he sent it back to me. Before they killed him, of course."

"Of course. Before they killed him." Now I understood.

"There's a note. It says, *Hey, sweetie, found this in a jar of nails. Tried to read it – it's gibberish. Figured it must be yours. Love, Danny.*"

"Well, that's great. But I don't think we should be talking about this."

"Why not?"

"On the phone, I mean."

"Oh, you mean, because of the ..." Her voice trailed off.

"Yeah."

"Then ... what?"

"How about you come down here for a visit?"

"To your place?"

"Uh-huh."

"Tonight?"

"No, tomorrow's good. And I need you to do me a favor, too. Go to Walmart and buy six flash drives and bring them with you. Okay?"

"Six? That's a lot."

"I'll pay you back," I said.

"You'd better."

I changed the subject. "How are you doing? You feeling all right?"

"I'm fine."

"The note from Danny didn't upset you?"

"Yeah, it did a little. I cried when I read it – he called me 'sweetie.' But I'm okay now. I told you, when I got upset before it was just because of the shock, because of the way I found out about, you know, Danny getting killed."

"All right. I'm glad you're feeling better. So, I'll see you tomorrow, then?"

"Yeah. Probably in the afternoon. I have to take my car in for service in the morning."

"What's wrong with it?"

"I don't know. The engine cuts in and out. The guy on the phone said it sounded like my something needed to be replaced."

"Your something?"

"Yeah, I forget what he called it. Anyway, I have an appointment to get it fixed at eleven. After that, I'll go to Walmart and get your stuff and then I'll come down to your place."

"Okay, that sounds good. See you then. Be careful."

"You, too." She said goodbye and hung up.

So, finally, it appeared we now had everything we needed to make sense of the notebooks. Teresa had the flash drive from Danny – the one with the copy of the notebooks on it – and I had the flash drive with the key to the code. We were, as the saying goes, back in business.

But a nagging thought had entered my mind while I was warning Teresa not to discuss this matter on the phone. If the government – or whoever was behind the attempts to keep us from finding out what was in the notebooks – was listening in on our phone calls, it was completely reasonable to think they might also have planted listening devices in our houses. Perhaps that's the reason they always seemed to be one step ahead of us.

Of course, the opposite could be true, as well. Maybe nothing was going on. Maybe it was all paranoia on the part of me and Teresa, and no one was trying to keep us from finding out what was in the notebooks. The break-ins, the thefts, Danny's death – all of it could have been just a series of strange coincidences. Except, there was one part of all this that had me convinced we weren't totally delusional – the fake alien.

Yeah, the fake alien. That was what tied all these 'strange coincidences' to the notebooks. There had to be a connection. Unless ...

A new possibility popped into my head, one I hadn't considered before. What if Teresa hadn't really seen an alien, fake or otherwise? What if it had all been a hallucination? After all, the intruders had shot her up with some kind of drug, and she didn't see the alien until after that happened. Maybe seeing the alien was a side effect of the drug they used.

After thinking about it for a while, I decided this last scenario was a little far-fetched. There were too many coincidences for this to be anything other than what we thought it was – someone, most likely some government agency, was actively working against us, trying to prevent us from succeeding. And they were even willing to commit murder as part of their scheme. Apparently, the notebooks contained explosive information not meant for public consumption, and they were prepared to do just about anything to prevent us from getting it.

There wasn't much I could do about that. The government's involvement, I mean. But there was something I *could* do – I could search my house for listening devices. Finding one would be the ultimate proof someone was trying to keep me and Teresa from discovering what was in the notebooks.

My ruminations were interrupted by rumblings from my stomach, reminding me humans cannot survive on a beer-only diet and that I hadn't had any solid food since breakfast at Teresa's, many hours ago. I went into the kitchen, popped a Hungry Man turkey dinner into my microwave, opened a fresh beer, sat down and formulated a plan for the evening – first I'd eat, then I'd search the house for bugs.

Chapter 11 – Starting Over

Over two hours of searching for listening devices turned up nothing. Of course, that didn't mean my house wasn't bugged. Government agents probably knew how to hide listening devices in places I'd never even think to look.

Or maybe there was nothing to find, because all this was little more than a slightly paranoid delusion on the part of me and Teresa. I'm sure that's what many smart people would have concluded, and I like to think of myself as a member of that group. Smart people, I mean. Still, someone like me, a writer with a slightly overactive imagination, might decide the opposite was true, that my opponent – whoever it was – was merely exceptionally good at hiding things. And finally, that's what I decided. Someone was behind all these strange happenings, and they were very good at their job.

It had been a long day and, despite my late-afternoon nap, I was tired. As I got ready for bed, worries about the new flash drive in my possession began to creep into my thoughts. Did our adversaries – the government, presumably – know I'd received it? What if there was an attempt to steal it? And what about Teresa, who was now back in possession of dead Jimmy's original flash drive? Was she also at risk?

I decided to take the flash drive to bed with me, tucking it under a corner of the fitted bottom sheet. It might not be difficult for an intruder to find, but no one could sneak in and steal it without me getting a good look at them, that was certain. Whether or not that would be a good thing, though, I wasn't sure.

I tossed and turned my way through the night, waking frequently and getting up a couple of times to investigate when I thought I heard noises outside. And also to relieve internal pressures caused by my previous day's consumption of too much beer. But, by the time daylight arrived, nothing bad had happened. I'd survived the night and I still had the flash drive.

According to an article I read a long time ago, if coffee didn't exist, a third of the workforce would not show up for work every day. That may or may not be true for the workforce, but it's gospel for me. Without my morning coffee – and lots of it – I am, basically, unable to function. So the first thing I did after stumbling out of the bathroom at seven o'clock was brew up a pot of hot, delicious java. I then fell asleep in my recliner and didn't wake up until almost nine. The day was off to a good start.

I wasted the rest of the day, getting absolutely nothing done, just sitting around, drinking coffee and waiting for Teresa to arrive so we could finally get an idea of what was in the notebooks. She finally showed up around two.

"It's about time," I said, as I let her in. "I thought you'd be in a hurry to get started on this."

"I *am* in a hurry. I probably would have been here at first light if I didn't have to take my car in. Since I didn't get any sleep at all last night."

"Me, either. So what was wrong with it?"

"I don't know. Something to do with the *accelerator module*, whatever that is. They had to replace it. Cost me 240 bucks."

"Ouch."

"Yeah, ouch. But it runs like a dream, now. " She tossed a plastic bag onto my kitchen table. "Your flash drives. The receipt's in the bag."

"Thanks."

"How old's that coffee?" she said.

"Second pot. Help yourself."

She got a mug out of my closet and poured herself a cup, then sat down at the kitchen table, across from me. "So, are you ready to get started?" She placed her flash drive – the one with the copy of the notebooks that Danny had inadvertently taken – in the center of the table.

"I am."

"Nervous?"

"Sure. Aren't you?"

"Yeah, I guess so. But excited, too," she said.

"Let me go get my computer," I said, getting up. "You wanna work here, or in the living room?"

"Here's good. I'll move over there and sit next to you."

"What else do you think we need?"

"Oh, I don't know. Maybe some scratch paper and pens." She paused, looking thoughtful. "You planning to print out any of this stuff?"

I hadn't thought of that but it seemed like a good idea. "Okay, I'll get my printer, too. Be right back." I went into my office – actually, just a corner of my bedroom that I've set up as an area for me to do my writing – and came back with my new computer, my laser printer, paper, pens, and, of course, the flash drive, dumping everything onto the table.

"So, how are we going to do this?" I said.

"It's up to you. This is your adventure – I'm just a sidekick." She grinned.

After a short discussion, we decided to copy both flash drives onto my computer and then print out the first five pages of each. Which we did, while we sat around making small talk, eating chocolate chip cookies from my stash of goodies, and drinking coffee.

"So that's your new computer?" Teresa said.

"Yeah."

"I need to get one, too."

"They've got tons of them at Walmart."

"I never heard of that brand. What is that? Kleizon?" She twisted her head around, attempting to read the upside-down letters on the front of my new laptop.

"Keizan," I said. "I never heard of it, either. It's Japanese, I think. Or maybe Korean."

"Aren't they all? How much?"

"About $375, with the tax."

"That's not too bad. Is it any good?"

"Seems okay, so far. But I haven't really used it for anything yet."

When we finally got the printed pages, I kept the five pages from *Interviews with Alien #1* and gave Teresa the corresponding five pages from the key to the code. The plan was to have me read out loud one letter at a time, whereupon Teresa would tell me the corresponding code letter and also write it down. Then, once we had a paragraph or two, we'd divide the letters, which had no space breaks between them, into words and see what it said.

But as I looked at the lines of nonsensical letters on my printed pages, I noticed something that had escaped my attention during my earlier perusal of the notebooks – a tiny, four-digit number embedded vertically in the middle of the third line of each paragraph. Each paragraph had a different number and the numbers were not sequential. The first paragraph on page one had the number 0017, for example, while paragraph two was 0009. However, when I looked at Teresa's page one, there was no number in her first paragraph. Or in any of her other paragraphs, either, for that matter.

We tried decoding the beginning of notebook one, matching the first paragraph of my page one against the first paragraph of Teresa's page one, but by the time we got to the end of the first line, we could see that wasn't working. All we got was a new line of random letters. Evidently, this wasn't going to be as easy as I'd originally anticipated.

It took us a while to figure it out. How to use the key, I mean. The secret was the numbers. A number in one of my paragraphs corresponded to the sequential number of a paragraph in the key. So, my paragraph one, with the number 0017, matched up with the 17th paragraph in the key, and my paragraph two, number 0009, was paragraph nine in the key. Of course, none of the paragraphs in the key were numbered, which meant we had to count through them to find the match.

"So, how do you want to do this?" Teresa said, after we'd finally solved the mystery of how the key worked.

"I guess we need to print out the entire key for notebook one, then go through it and number each paragraph."

"That's going to take a while."

"Yeah, it is."

"Why did he do it like that? Make it so complicated?"

"It looks as if the code changes with each paragraph, that every time there's a new paragraph, there's a new code to go with it. That would make it just about impossible to break the code without the key. You need lots of words to break a code – one little paragraph isn't close to enough."

"I guess Uncle Bill wouldn't have been much help, then."

"Probably not. Not even the NSA could break a code like this." I looked at my watch. Almost five-thirty. "You hungry?" I said.

"A little. Not *super* hungry, though."

"I've got some frozen dinners – mostly turkey and chicken. Or I could run into town and get some burgers or pizza or something."

"I could eat a burger," she said.

"Okay." I checked the amount of paper in my printer, added some and started printing out the remaining pages of *Interviews with Alien #1*. "Be back in about 15 minutes," I said, grabbing my keys off the kitchen counter.

"And get some beer!" she yelled after me as I closed the door and headed down the steps.

Chapter 12 – A Difficult Job

The pages had finished printing and Teresa was hard at work, numbering the paragraphs, when I got back. I deposited burgers, fries, Cokes and two sundaes – chocolate fudge for me and caramel for her – on the table and wedged a 12-pack into my crowded refrigerator. I ought to clean this fridge out pretty soon, I thought, as a slightly unpleasant aroma wafted toward me from its overpacked interior.

"Put the sundaes in the freezer," Teresa said. "We can eat them later."

I added the sundaes to the freezer, barely managing to squeeze them in among the frozen dinners, cartons of ice cream, breakfast sandwiches, and layers of ice that coated the interior. The odor from the refrigerator below was present up here, too. I mentally added defrosting the freezer to my *to do someday soon* list.

We took our food into the living room and ate there, sitting on my ratty old couch with our feet propped up on my equally ratty-looking coffee table. "You wanna watch the local news?" I said. "It's six o'clock."

"Sure. Whatever."

I turned on one of the Tampa stations and we sat there, eating and watching the daily accounting of home invasions, carjackings, shootings and serious traffic accidents. All the bad news reminded me of why I liked living in Fort Meade, a peaceful little community only 40 or 50 miles from the crime and traffic of Tampa Bay. The last big crime I remember happening here was about eight years ago, when someone stole a bicycle and left it 10 blocks away. People in town were shocked! And traffic – well, there just isn't any.

When the weather came on, I turned off the TV. "We need to get back to work," I said.

"Don't you want to see the weather?"

"No. I already know what the weather's going to be."

"Really?"

"Yes. Tomorrow, cloudy in the morning, sunny in the early afternoon with a high chance of thunder and lightning in the late afternoon. Odds that it'll rain are about 50-50. Same for the day after tomorrow and the day after that and every day until October."

"Amazing. I never knew you were the weather psychic," Teresa said, laughing.

"Just one of my many, many talents."

We went back into the kitchen and Teresa resumed numbering the paragraphs on the printout. There wasn't much I could do until she was finished because some of the early paragraphs in my encoded version had numbers higher than 1,500. So I sat across the table and watched her as she whipped through page after page, numbering the paragraphs. When she was finished she said, "Whew!"

"How many?" I said.

"One thousand, six hundred and forty-three paragraphs."

"Wow, that's a lot."

"Yeah, and this is only the first notebook."

"I know. Gotta do it, though, if we want to figure out what they say."

"I guess. I just hope this is all worth it, that the notebooks have some really incredible information – *new* information, not the same old stuff that's in every science fiction book out there."

"Well, let's start decoding and find out," I said.

We worked until 11 o'clock, by which time we had decoded only the first four pages. And they were a huge disappointment. They contained no information about aliens or, for that fact, any interesting information at all. Basically, all we had was a *disclaimer* from dead Jimmy, wherein he advised that everything in the notebook could be completely wrong because the information was all based on his *interpretation* of images that were placed into his head from external sources – by alien #1, presumably. There was also a brief biography of Jimmy, some information about his training and, finally, a caution that he couldn't vouch for the veracity of *any* of the information he'd obtained. It was, he said, entirely possible that aliens were liars!

"I'm pooped," said Teresa. "This is hard work." She leaned back in her chair and stretched out her arms above her head, interlocking the fingers of her hands and throwing in a slight groan, for emphasis.

"I agree. And we didn't even learn anything interesting."

"We'll probably get into the good stuff next time. Meanwhile, I've gotta get going. We can get together tomorrow and continue working on this, I guess. If you want to, that is."

"You're going home?"

"Uh-huh. It's late. Ladies need their beauty sleep, you know."

"Why don't you spend the night?" I said.

"Stay over?"

"Sure. Why not? There isn't anything you have to do up in Bartow, tomorrow, is there? Like go to work, maybe?"

"No. My boss told me to take a couple of weeks off."

"Nice boss."

"You're right. He is."

"So, . . .? We'll get more done if we're not running back and forth between here and your place."

"Yeah, okay, I guess. That sounds all right."

"I'll even make breakfast," I said.

"In that case, I'm not gonna stay," she said, laughing. "I've had your cooking before."

"That bad, huh?"

"Yup."

"I've got microwaveable breakfast sandwiches. Even I can't screw those up."

"Are you sure?" She gave me a dubious look.

"Pretty sure. We'll find out in the morning," I said, grinning. "What time do you wanna get up?"

"Oh, ... sometime around noon would be good."

"Okay, then. Seven-thirty it is."

She stuck her tongue out at me. "Can I borrow a toothbrush?"

"You're going to bed now?"

"Yeah. It's already past my regular bedtime. Usually I have to get up and go to work, you know."

In my bedroom closet is an old shoebox labeled *Teeth*. Inside the box are about a dozen toothbrushes, several small tubes of toothpaste, some dental floss, and a couple of sample bottles of mouthwash, all of it courtesy of my dental hygienist, who gives me a bag full of these sample products every time I get my teeth cleaned. I grabbed one of each item, along with some towels, and put them in the bathroom across the hall from the guest bedroom.

"Did I leave any clothes here?" called Teresa from the kitchen.

"There are still some things in the bedroom," I yelled back.

We passed each other in the hall as I headed back to the kitchen. "Aren't you going to bed?" she said.

"Nah, I think I'm going to watch TV for a while and try to forget all this alien stuff."

"Okay, then. See you tomorrow. About noon, right?"

"Sure. And if you get lonely in the middle of the night..."

"What? Call my sister?"

I grinned. "Yeah, that's what I meant – call your sister."

She leaned up and kissed me on the cheek. "Goodnight," she said.

"See you in the morning." I went into the living room, flopped into my recliner and turned on the TV, tuning into *Jimmy Kimmel Live!*. After Jimmy did his monologue, I began searching through the channel guide, looking to see what else was on, and discovered one of my all time favorite movies, *Rear Window*, was just about to start. Although I'd seen it before – several times, in fact – it had been years since the last time. I changed the channel, got a beer from the fridge, and made myself comfortable.

I've never really been much of a movie fan, but I like just about everything Alfred Hitchcock ever directed. And while *Rear Window* wouldn't be number one on my list of Hitchcock films – that would be *North by Northwest* – it was still a great flick. I settled back to watch.

I guess I got too comfortable in my recliner because, at some point early in the film, I fell asleep. That happens to me a lot, actually. Falling asleep in front of the TV, I mean. There's just something about television that makes me sleepy. Anyway, I was still there, in my recliner, fast asleep, when Teresa's phone rang at 6:15 the next morning, waking me up.

Chapter 13 – Boom!

Teresa's phone rang several times, stopped, then rang again before she answered. "Hello," she said, her voice groggy with sleep. There was a pause, followed by, "Yes. This is Teresa Ruiz."

I sat up, curious. Or nosy, as some might say. My back was stiff from my night in the recliner.

"What?" she said, and then, after a slight delay, "WHAT!!"

That didn't sound good. I wondered what was going on.

"Tell me this is a joke," she said.

At this point, Teresa went into the bathroom across the hall and shut the door, leaving me unable to hear the rest of the conversation. But whatever the phone call was about, it didn't sound as if we'd be getting back to sleep. I went into the kitchen and made a pot of coffee.

"What was that all about?" I said, when she joined me in the kitchen.

"You're not going to believe this," she said. "My house blew up!"

"What?" I was sure I must have heard her incorrectly.

"That was the Bartow police. My house exploded. They think it was a gas leak."

"You're kidding me," I said.

She shook her head. "Nope. It's funny, though."

"What's funny about your house exploding?"

"Not funny ha ha, funny *strange*. My house doesn't have gas, everything's electric."

Hmm, that *was* strange. Although actually, once I thought about it, I already knew Teresa's house was all-electric. After all, at one time – back when she and I were romantically involved – I spent almost as much time there as I did at my own house.

And if her house didn't use gas, what caused it to go boom? I could think of only three reasons why houses in the United States exploded – gas leaks, methamphetamine labs, and bombings. So, it wasn't a gas leak and I was pretty sure Teresa wasn't cooking meth in a back room somewhere. That meant someone had deliberately blown up her house.

"I've got to go home," she said.

"Sit down and have a cup of coffee, first."

She sat down at the table and I poured us each a mug of coffee. "The police want me to come in for an interview," she said, blowing on her coffee and taking a tentative sip. "And I want to see what's left of my house."

"Drink your coffee and then I'll go with you. And we'll go by your house and take a look."

"Okay."

"What time do you have to be there? At the police station, I mean."

"Whenever I want, I guess. They told me to come in at my earliest convenience."

"Great. Are you hungry?"

"No."

"I've got sausage, egg and cheese sandwiches," I said. "On croissants."

"Thanks, but I don't have much of an appetite. And my house blew up!"

I couldn't think of any comforting words to say to that so I took a sip of my coffee and nodded.

"It's lucky I wasn't home," she said.

"Yeah. *Really* lucky."

"You think it was them?"

"Who else?"

"Boy, someone really doesn't want us to see what's in those notebooks. Do you think they were trying to kill me?"

"No, I don't think so."

"Why not? They killed Danny."

"I think if they wanted to kill you, you'd be dead."

Teresa's body gave a little shudder – I probably shouldn't have been so blunt. She took a drink of her coffee, then said, "I guess you're right, it must have been a warning. Anyone could see I wasn't home. My house was all dark and my car was gone."

"Some warning, blowing up your house," I said. "You know, it's not too late for you to back out of this. Just forget about all this alien and notebook nonsense and go back to your normal life."

"Are you kidding? Go back to my *normal* life? After they killed Danny and blew up my house? Not a *fucking* chance!"

I was shocked. I'd never heard Teresa swear before – at least, not using *that* word. Obviously, she was a lot angrier than her outward appearance revealed.

"And we don't even know who *they* are," she said.

"It's has to be the government. Somebody – some government agency – doesn't want us to decode those notebooks and see what they say."

"Yeah. Gotta be. They've been covering up UFOs and aliens for years. I'll bet the notebooks contain proof they exist – that's why they don't want us to see it."

"Maybe," I said, but to myself I was thinking, *Definitely*.

I brought out my stash of chocolate chip cookies and we sat there for another hour or so, not talking all that much, just nibbling on cookies and drinking coffee. In spite of her continuing protestations of not being hungry, Teresa managed to eat almost as many cookies as I did. When we ran out of cookies, I poured the rest of the coffee into a travel mug and we got ready to leave.

"Do you think they'll blow up your house while we're gone?" Teresa said, as we were heading out the door.

"I sure hope not. But at least we've got the flash drives with us, if they do."

"You know, you don't have to go with me. I can do this by myself. You could stay here and guard your house."

"I don't think I want to be here if they blow up my house," I said.

"Yeah, I can see where that might be a problem," she said, nodding her head.

We took my car. It was after nine when we got to Bartow. We swung by Teresa's to check on the damage to her house. It was extensive, but describing it as the police had – *Your house blew up* – might have been a bit much. Basically, the house didn't explode, it was the garage. But the explosion had severely damaged the garage-side of the house, and it looked as if there had been a small fire.

Several police and firemen were still at the scene, which was surrounded by yellow police tape. That meant no one except cops and firefighters were allowed on the property, as we found out when we ducked under the tape and attempted to approach the house. A police officer stopped us.

"You folks can't come in here," he said. "It's a crime scene."

"This is my house," said Teresa. She held out her driver's license for the officer to inspect.

He took her license, looked at it briefly and then gave it back. "I'm sorry, ma'am. But we haven't finished our investigation, and you can't come in until we're done."

"Do you know when that will be?" she said.

"No, ma'am, I don't. But it shouldn't be too much longer."

"Is the inside of my house badly damaged?"

"Well, not so much the inside. But the garage, as you can see, is completely destroyed."

"Yeah, we can see that. It's gone." All that was left of the garage were several small piles of rubble and splintered wood scattered about the lot.

"Most of the damage inside is in the kitchen area. Broken dishes and stuff on the floor, and there was a small fire. There's some water damage from when they put that out."

"Great," Teresa said.

"It's not too bad," the cop said. "Though you're probably going to need to get some carpentry work done and you'll definitely need new appliances."

"Appliances?"

"You know. Stove, refrigerator, like that. They were damaged in the fire."

"Oh. Anything else?"

"That's about it. The fire department has a structural engineer checking out the house, just to make sure it's safe to occupy. Once we're finished and he's finished, we'll remove the tape and you can get back into your house."

We thanked the cop for the information, ducked under the tape and headed back to my car. "Blowing up my house. Damn. This is *really* starting to piss me off," Teresa said.

"Just starting?"

"No. I already was pissed off at these guys. Whoever they are. But now I'm *really* pissed off."

I nodded. "I can understand why."

"Anyway, let's go see what they want at the police station."

Chapter 14 – Questions, Questions, Questions

Our interview with the Bartow Police did not go well. At all. They seemed, ... well, I think *suspicious* is the only word that would accurately describe their attitudes.

Two officers took us into an interview room – not an interrogation room or anything like that, just an undecorated room with comforting green walls, a long table surrounded by a half-dozen chairs, and not much else, other than a three-year-old calendar with pictures of kittens, hanging by the door. At first, they weren't going to let me accompany Teresa, but when she insisted, telling them I knew just as much about what was going on as she did, they changed their minds. We took seats on one side of the table and the two cops – Officers Jensen and Sweeney – sat opposite us.

Officer Jensen placed a notebook, a pen and a digital recorder on the table. He turned on the recorder. "Do you have any objections to us recording this interview?" he said.

Teresa looked at me and then back at Officer Jensen. "No," she said

My turn. "Would it make a difference if I did?" I said.

"Officer Jensen smiled. "Not really."

"Then no, I guess."

"All right. Please state your names for the record."

We gave him our names and other pertinent information, that being mainly about how the two of us were connected. Both officers seemed skeptical of our claims that we were just *friends*.

"But Ms. Ruiz spent last night at your house in Fort Meade, correct?" Officer Jensen said to me.

"Yes," I said, not adding any clarification, which was obviously what he was seeking.

"I see."

Throughout all this, the other officer – Sweeney – never said a word. He just sat there, across from us, an unfriendly, distrustful look on his face. It was almost as if he thought *we* were the ones who blew up Teresa's house.

"So," Officer Jensen began, "we have reason to believe your house was bombed, blown up on purpose."

"Bombed? Then why did you tell me on the phone it was a gas leak?"

"That wasn't me. That was someone with preliminary, but inaccurate information."

"Obviously. My house doesn't have gas."

"We know that." He paused. "Which brings us back to the fact that someone blew up your house. Your garage, actually, but the house was also damaged. Do you have any idea who might have done that?"

"Yes."

"Yes?" Officer Jensen seemed surprised at Teresa's answer. He leaned forward, his suddenly-increased interest apparent. Officer Sweeney remained silent and continued to glare at us.

"Yes, I do. I'm pretty sure I know who blew up my house – my garage."

"And who might that be?"

"The government."

Judging by the look on Officer Jensen's face, this was not the answer he was expecting. He looked briefly at his partner, as if seeking an explanation, then back at Teresa. "The U.S. Government?"

"I'm assuming," she said.

"So, you don't know for sure?"

"No. I can't prove it, if that's what you mean. But you asked me if I had any idea who might have done it, and I think it was the government."

"And why do you think that?"

"Well, because I'm in possession of something they don't want me to have and they've been trying to get it back. Did you know my house was burglarized recently?"

"Yes. I saw that, earlier. Two people broke in, right? And stole only one item. Your computer."

"Yeah. My computer. My beautiful, expensive computer."

I guess that last part was to back up Teresa's earlier claim that her computer cost $1800.

"Was that the government, too?" Officer Jensen wanted to know.

"Yeah, I think so."

"And what is this 'something' the government is trying to, uh, steal from you?"

"It's information."

"That was on your computer?"

"Yes."

"Exactly what kind of information is this? Is this something you obtained illegally?"

"Of course not. If I obtained it illegally, the government wouldn't have to *steal* it back, would they? They'd just have me arrested and *take* it back. This is information they're trying to suppress."

"I see. So, what is it? The information."

"You're going to find this hard to believe."

"It's fine. I've heard lots of strange stories. Go ahead."

"It's about aliens."

"Okay. Illegal aliens. What else?"

"Not 'illegal' aliens – outer space aliens. Little grays."

"What?" was the reaction from Officer Jensen. Even his partner reacted. He chortled and said, "Huh! Aliens!"

"I told you this was hard to believe," Teresa said.

Officer Jensen regained his composure and said, "All right. So, this information on your computer was about aliens? Outer space aliens?"

"Yes."

"What did it say, the information?"

"I don't know."

"You don't know what the information on your computer said?"

"That's right. It was encoded. That's the way we got it from dead Jimmy."

The words 'dead Jimmy' seemed to get both officers' attention. "Did you say, '*dead* Jimmy?'" said Officer Sweeney.

"Yeah," said Teresa.

Officer Jensen fixed his partner with a look that said, "*I'm* the one doing the questioning, here. *You* should be quiet and observe."

Officer Sweeney was apparently skilled at reading looks from his partner. He leaned back, away from the table, and resumed glaring at us.

"So, just who is Jimmy and why is he dead?" said Officer Jensen.

"I should probably answer that," I said.

"All right. Go ahead."

"Well, Jimmy Chisholm was a guy I went to school with, a long, long time ago," I said, and I proceeded to relate the story of Jimmy's death while at language school and then me getting a phone call from him some 40 years later, telling me he was an alien interpreter.

"I see. Okay, he talks to aliens and then he writes notes in these books. And he wants to send them to you, right?"

"Yeah. And he did. Three notebooks. Big, industrial-size notebooks."

"And you refer to him as 'dead Jimmy' because of what happened at the language school back when you were students there?"

"Right."

"So, now you've got the notebooks. And this is the same information that was on Ms. Ruiz's computer that was stolen?"

"Yes. There was a flash drive in the box with the notebooks, with the same information. So I gave it to her and she copied it onto her computer."

"What happened to the flash drive?" Officer Jensen said.

"It was still plugged into the port in my computer when they stole it," said Teresa, picking up the narrative.

"So the flash drive was taken, too?"

"Yes," said Teresa.

"And all the information was in a secret code? Which you couldn't decode?"

"That's right."

"I don't quite understand how stealing your computer and then blowing up your garage actually accomplishes anything for whoever did this?" said Officer Jensen. He turned his attention back to me. "If you still have the notebooks and –"

"I don't," I said, interrupting him.

"You don't? What happened to them?"

I told him the story of how I came back from Teresa's to find my door ajar and the notebooks and my computer missing.

"Did you report the theft?" he said.

"No, I didn't."

"Why not?"

"We don't have police in Fort Meade."

"There's a sheriff's sub-station. You could have reported it there."

"I suppose. But I didn't."

"So, at this point, everything's gone?"

"Well, not everything. Teresa still had a copy of the notebooks on a flash drive."

"I thought that was stolen along with her computer."

"No. This is a different flash drive. A copy she made and hid in her garage." I decided to leave out the part about Danny taking the flash drive and then getting killed after sending it back to us. This story was complicated enough without adding in a related murder.

"I see," said Officer Jensen, even though the look on his face belied his words. "So, ... let me see if I've got this straight. The notebooks are gone, but you still have a copy of them on a flash drive. Except, you can't read what it says because it's encoded and you don't have the key. Is that right?"

"That's about it," I said. Of course, that last part was a lie – we *did* have the key to break the code. However, I felt it wiser not to mention that we soon would be able to read what was on the flash drive. The less people who knew that fact, the safer I felt.

Officer Sweeney continued to glare at us. I began to wonder if there was something wrong with him – something that made him always look mean and disgusted. A genetic mutation, maybe, like those grouchy-looking cats you see on YouTube.

Officer Jensen returned to questioning Teresa, trying to make sense of our story. While he did that, I turned my attention to the lobby area, which I could see through the glass top-half of the door. Something very unusual was happening out there. Tommy Lee Jones, looking exactly as he did in those *Men in Black* movies – you know, with the black suit and the sunglasses – was having a conversation with two officers. As I watched them, he pointed in our direction and the officers turned to look. I quickly averted my gaze.

What the hell was going on? What was Tommy Lee Jones doing in Bartow, Florida, in the police station, shooting the breeze with a couple of cops? And was time travel involved? The Tommy Lee Jones in the lobby was at least 20 years younger than he should have been.

The door opened and another officer came in. He leaned over, cupped his hand around Officer Jensen's left ear and whispered something to him. He then nodded at Officer Sweeney and the two of them left, leaving the door open.

"Well, I guess I have everything I need for now," said Officer Jensen. He leaned forward and turned off his recorder. "If we have any more questions, we'll be in touch."

"That's it?" said Teresa.

"That's it. If you have any problems, feel free to give us a call." He handed a business card to Teresa, then scooped up his notebook, pen and recorder and started to leave. "Oh, one more thing," he said, turning back."

"Yes?"

"Since this case is, ... uh, how shall I say? *Unusual*? Feel free to have your insurance company give me a call at that number if they have any questions." He pointed at the card he'd just given Teresa.

"Okay. Thanks."

And that was that. Our interview was over. Officer Jensen left and so did we. And, although I looked for him, Tommy Lee Jones was nowhere in sight as we left the station.

"That was really strange," Teresa said, as we walked across the parking lot toward my car. "The way he ended the interview right after that other officer came in. I thought he was just about to ask me if he could get a copy of the flash drive."

"You don't know the half of it," I said, and proceeded to tell her what I'd seen out in the lobby.

"Really?" she said. "Tommy Lee Jones? Men in Black? Time travel?"

I unlocked the car and we got in. "Maybe. Who knows what the hell is going on?" I started her up and eased the old Buick out onto the highway and into traffic.

"Yeah, I guess you're right. Who knows?" said Teresa. "But I know one thing."

"What's that?"

"This case – this ... *thing* we're involved in – just gets stranger and stranger."

I couldn't argue with that.

Chapter 15 – And More Questions

We decided, after a brief but friendly argument, that Teresa would stay at my place while she arranged for repair work on her house, so we headed over to her house to pick up some of her clothes and other personal items. The police and the crime scene tape were gone. I parked in the driveway – being careful to avoid the rubble – and we went in the house. The place was a mess.

Damage was much worse than that policeman had described to us when we were here earlier. The kitchen was pretty much destroyed from a combination of the blast hitting that side of the house, the resultant fire, and water damage from the firefighters' efforts to extinguish it. There was also some light smoke damage in other parts of the house and a minor amount of water damage in the living room.

"What a mess," was all Teresa had to say, after we'd finished our inspection.

"Yeah, it's a mess, all right. I hope you have good insurance," I said.

"I do. Or, at least, I *think* I do. We'll find out when I call them."

"All right. So let's get what you need and be on our way. There's nothing we can do here."

"Okay." She disappeared into her bedroom, emerging a few minutes later with an armful of clothes. "This should be enough," she said.

We locked the house and Teresa left a note on the front door, saying she was staying with a friend and including my phone number. While she was doing that, I put her clothes into the back seat of my car. "Ready?" I said.

"Yup." She took a final look around and got into the car.

"Then away we go," I said, trying to sound cheerful. I started to back out of the driveway, but before I could, a police car pulled in behind me, blocking our exit. The cop car hit us with a one-second chirp of its siren, warning us it was there. I stopped, shifted into *Park* and shut off the engine.

Two officers got out of the police car and approached us. One of them stayed behind my car and the other approached the driver's side window. His hand rested lightly on the butt of his still-holstered gun. *Now what?* I wondered.

"Howdy," said the cop as I lowered my window. His name tag identified him as Officer O'Brien and his puffy red face confirmed his Irish heritage.

I smiled up at him. "Hi."

"Can I see your license and proof of insurance?" he said. Technically, I guess, it was a question, but it sounded like a command.

"Sure." I pulled out my wallet, took out my license and insurance card and handed them to him.

He looked them over and said, "And what are we doing here today?"

"Just picking up some clothes." I indicated the clothes in the back seat with a nod of my head.

"I see that," said the cop, glancing into my back seat. "Did you know this is a crime scene?"

"I believe it's been released. The yellow tape has been removed."

"And that looting is a serious crime?" the cop continued, ignoring my answer.

"Looting?" I said.

Teresa leaned forward in her seat and faced the cop. "Hey! We're not looting," she said. "This is *my* house and these are *my* clothes!"

Officer O'Brien leaned down so he could get a better look at Teresa. "Ma'am?" he said.

"I live here. This is my house – I own it!"

"May I see some identification, please?" he said.

Teresa passed her driver's license to me and I gave it to Officer O'Brien. He looked at it briefly, then said, "Just a second," and headed back to where his partner was waiting.

I could see the two cops conversing in my rear-view mirror. Officer O'Brien handed our licenses to his partner, who looked at them and then disappeared from my mirror in the direction of the patrol car. I guess the plan was to check out our story.

"You don't look like a looter," I said to Teresa, attempting to make light of the situation.

She punched me gently in the right shoulder. "It's *you*! You're the one who looks like a looter, not me."

I laughed, just as Officer O'Brien reappeared at my window.

"Something funny?" he said.

I smiled at him. "It's personal. A joke."

He didn't smile back. "So. Let me see if I understand this. You two live here together and – "

"No, no," I said. "I don't live here. I live at the address on my license."

"In Fort Meade?"

"Yes. And Teresa, here, is my friend and she's going to stay with me while the house gets repaired. So we were just picking up some stuff to take to my place."

"I see."

"We just came from the police station," Teresa said.

"Ma'am?"

"We just came from being interviewed at the the police station."

"Interviewed? Both of you?"

"Yes."

"Who conducted the interview?"

Teresa shrugged. "I don't know. Two cops. Officer Jenkins, something like that. I forget the other guy's name."

"It was Jensen," I said, correcting her. "Officer Jensen asked the questions and the other officer was named Sweeney. He just observed."

Officer O'Brien's face brightened. "Oh. Sweetness."

"What?" said both Teresa and myself at the same time.

"Bob Sweeney. Sweetness. That's his nickname."

How appropriate, I thought. But I said nothing and neither did Teresa.

The other cop returned and handed our licenses to his partner, who then handed them back to me. They exchanged a few quiet words away from the window, then Officer O'Brien leaned down and said,

"Everything checks out. Sorry for the delay, but we have to make sure you are who you say you are."

"Well, we are," said Teresa, sounding slightly miffed.

"Yes, ma'am. And I am sorry. But we've been instructed by the department to keep an eye on your house, just in case ... well, in case there *are* looters. So a patrol car is coming by here every half-hour or so."

"Well, thank you for that," she said, softening her tone. "I appreciate it."

"You're welcome, ma'am."

"May I ask you a question?" I said.

"Certainly," Officer O'Brien said.

"You ever see any of those *Men in Black* movies?"

"Yes, sir. I've seen all three of them."

"Great. Is there someone in the department – at the police station – who looks like Tommy Lee Jones did in those movies? You know, black suit, white shirt, black tie – a man in black."

He looked thoughtful for a few seconds, then said, "Offhand, I can't think of anyone."

"Oh." I guess I was expecting him to say yes. "All right. Thanks."

"You want me to ask my partner?"

"No, that's okay. It's fine. And we've got to get going."

Officer O'Brien lightly slapped the roof of my car. "You're good to go, then. Don't forget to fasten your seat belts. And drive safely. Have a good day."

"You, too," I said, but even as I said it, a few drops of rain hit my windshield. I leaned forward and looked up at the sky. Ominous, inky-dark clouds were forming south of Bartow, which meant we were likely to be driving right into a huge thunderstorm on the way back to Fort Meade. It did not look as if any of us – me, Teresa, and the two cops – were going to have a 'good day.'

"It's going to rain," I announced.

"Really?" said Teresa, a slightly amused expression on her face as the intensity of the raindrops hitting the windshield increased. "The weather psychic strikes again. He's amazing!"

I smiled at her. "You wanna go get something to eat and wait 'til the storm blows over?"

"Oh, ... I don't know. What about you?"

"Up to you."

"Let's just go home – back to your place, I mean – and I'll make us something to eat. Maybe I'll even clean out that stinky refrigerator of yours."

"That would be great. I've been meaning to do that," I said.

Teresa laughed. "Yeah, since when? A year ago Christmas?"

"That sounds about right." As I backed out of the driveway and we headed for Fort Meade, the rain started coming down in wind-blown sheets. It looked as if this storm was a bit more than the usual thunderstorm, and might be around for a while.

Chapter 16 – The FBI

We were home for less than an hour when Tommy Lee Jones, still dressed in his *Men in Black* attire, knocked on my kitchen door. Teresa was in the guest room, putting away her clothes and rearranging the room to suit her taste. I answered the door.

"Mr. Novicki?" he said.

"Yes, that's me," I said, a little taken aback to find him standing on the covered landing outside my door, shaking off the moisture from an umbrella. I hadn't heard him drive in, probably because of all the noise from the rain and the thunder.

"Senior Special Agent Marvin Keglar, FBI," he said, introducing himself. He flashed a badge at me – much too quickly for me to get a good look at it. "I have a couple of questions I'd like to ask you. Do you mind?"

It didn't seem like a good idea to 'mind' answering questions from a slightly-wet FBI agent standing at my door, so I said, "No. No, I don't mind. You wanna come in?" Fortunately, Teresa and I had not yet started our decoding session for the day and no telltale evidence of our activities lay about the kitchen.

"Thank you." He wiped his feet on the welcome mat outside the door. Then, noticing the large dog dish and chain on the landing, he paused. "You have a dog?" he said.

"No, no, I don't. Those are just, uh, burglar deterrents."

"Very clever." He wiped his feet again, leaned his umbrella against the railing and came inside. "Do they work?"

"Well, not so much, lately," I said, remembering the break-in that cost me the notebooks and my computer.

He nodded, as if he was aware of my recent history. "May I sit?" he said, indicating a chair by the kitchen table.

"Please. You want some coffee? Or a beer?"

"No, thank you." He took a seat. "I'm fine. And this won't take long. Like I said, just a couple of questions."

I sat down across from him. Up close, I could see he didn't look at all like the star of the *Men in Black* movies. It must have been the outfit – a black suit, a white shirt and a black tie could make just about any middle-aged man look like Tommy Lee Jones, I decided.

It was at about this time that Teresa came back to the kitchen. "What's going on?" she said, eyeing the two of us, sitting at the kitchen table.

Agent Keglar stood and introduced himself. He seemed to know who Teresa was, even though she hadn't been introduced to him, as he called her by name when he said, "Won't you join us at the table, Ms. Ruiz? I have some questions for you, too."

"Are you one of those men in black guys?" she said, not sitting down. That's one of the things I always liked about Teresa – her directness.

Agent Keglar looked surprised, and then amused. "You mean, like in the movies?"

"Exactly."

"No. I am who I said I was, Senior Special Agent Marvin Keglar, and I work for the Federal Bureau of Investigation."

"You're a field agent?"

"Yes."

"And you go around trying to scare people after they've seen a UFO, right?"

Senior Special Agent Keglar of the FBI laughed. "No, I don't do that. I investigate crimes, arrest bad guys, stuff like that."

With a dubious look on her face, Teresa finally sat down at the table.

"I was hoping to get a chance to speak with you in Bartow – at the police station – but you left before I had the chance," Agent Keglar began.

"Sorry." I said.

"You said you had questions. What are they?" said Teresa, getting right to the point.

"Well, ..."

"Are you investigating us?"

Agent Keglar smiled at Teresa. "Investigating? I guess you could say the two of you are a point of interest."

"Point of interest? What's that mean?"

"We – actually, just me, for the time being – I'm looking into, how shall I put it, the *strange* goings-on around you two, lately."

"You mean the break-ins and stuff, right?"

"Yes. The break-ins, the explosion at your house, the death of your ex-husband, –"

"Danny? You're investigating Danny's murder, too?"

That was interesting. Special Agent Keglar knowing about what had happened to Danny, I mean. We deliberately hadn't mentioned Danny's death to the Bartow police and, as far as I knew, no one around here had made the connection between that and what was happening locally. The only way anyone could have known about it was to have been a party to the phone conversation between Teresa and Investigator Tellis Mims. Like I was.

"Yes, your ex-husband's murder is part of it," Agent Keglar said. "However, it's not exactly an investigation. I'm just –"

"Yeah, yeah, I know. Looking into things."

"Yes."

"It sounds like an investigation, to me," Teresa said.

"Well, you can call it that, if you like."

"I *do* like."

"That's fine," Agent Keglar said, and smiled. If Teresa was trying to annoy him, or make him lose his temper, it wasn't working. He just sat there, a pleasant look on his face, calm and patient, answering her questions and asking his own.

Actually, it was a little difficult to tell who was in charge of the questioning – every time Agent Keglar would mention something or ask a question, Teresa would respond with a question of her own. I leaned back in my chair and watched in admiration as the two of them bantered back and forth. So many questions came from Teresa – was it possible that, somewhere along the way, unbeknown to me, she'd been trained as a lawyer?

"So, what about Danny?" she said.

"I've spoken to Investigator Mims, up in Bay County, about what happened. He seems to think this was a robbery gone bad."

"Uh-huh. That's what he told me, too."

"Do you know what they – the robbers – were looking for? Were they after some particular item, do you think?"

"Like what?"

"I don't know. I'm asking you."

"I have no idea," Teresa said. "Investigator Mims said they took everything. All Danny's tools and stuff. Doesn't that mean they weren't after any specific item? That it was just a regular old robbery?"

"Maybe. Or maybe that's what they wanted it to look like."

"They? Who's *they*?"

"The robbers, of course. So, you don't know of anything special the robbers might have been after?"

"Nope."

"Why, exactly, were you trying to contact your ex-husband, anyway?" Agent Keglar said.

"Well, we're still friends. We stay in touch. So, I gave him a call one day and his phone was out of service. When I couldn't reach him by phone, we went up to Dade City to see him. But he wasn't there, so I stuck a note on his door and we left."

"The two of you?" He pointed at me, then at Teresa, then back at me.

"Yes."

"This would be the time you encountered the next-door neighbor?"

"You know about that?"

"Yes."

"This really sounds like an investigation. You talking to Danny's neighbor and all."

"I actually never spoke to him, but I did receive a copy of a report he filed with the local sheriff's office. Apparently, he's the head of the local Neighborhood Watch and he found the two of you to be a little suspicious."

"It still sounds like an investigation to me," Teresa said.

"All right. Fine. It's an investigation." For the first time, a hint of annoyance crept into Agent Keglar's voice.

The two of them continued their back-and-forth. It became obvious to me what was going on. Senior Special Agent Marvin Keglar of the FBI wasn't just 'looking into' a couple of odd break-ins. For some reason – most likely something to do with our possession of the notebooks – he was investigating *us*. And now he wanted to know why we hadn't told the Bartow Police about Danny's murder.

It was also pretty clear he already knew about the notebooks, the flash drives, and the rest of our story – minus the fact that we now had a copy of the code, of course – even though he hadn't mentioned them. After all, he'd been in the police station while we were there and he appeared to have been the one who put an end to our interview. And all the rest of the information could have come from normal, legitimate channels. So the government – or, at least, the FBI – really had no need to be breaking into our houses or blowing them up or killing Danny. They could have just arrested us and hauled everything away as *evidence*. But, if it wasn't the FBI, who was it?

"Oh. I get it," I blurted out.

Agent Keglar turned his attention to me. "Get what?" he said.

I actually hadn't meant to say that out loud, but I had. Now I needed to explain it. "I was just putting all this together," I said. "About what's going on, where you fit into it, how you have all this information about us. Before, I thought you – the FBI, I mean – might have been involved in these things that have been happening to us. But now I see you could have gotten all this info from other agencies and stuff."

Agent Keglar smiled his most disarming smile. "Of course. What did you think? That we'd tapped your phone or bugged your house? Something like that?"

"No. No, of course not," I lied. "That thought never even entered my head."

Chapter 17 – A Bad Good Idea

Special Agent Keglar's 'couple of questions' took almost two hours, thanks to Teresa's constant challenges and our unwillingness to provide him with the answers he was seeking. But eventually he left, slogging through the wind and the rain out to his car as pieces of Spanish moss from nearby oak trees blew about my driveway, threatening to attack him. Black clouds continued to dominate the sky. This was not your typical mid-to-late-afternoon, central Florida thunderstorm.

We sat in the kitchen, eating cookies and drinking coffee while we discussed what had just happened. It turned out Teresa had lied when she promised to make us 'something to eat' when we got home. But, at my house, there's always cookies!

"You don't think he'll come back, do you?" Teresa said, a worried look darkening her face.

"Come back? Why would he do that?"

"You know, like Columbo."

"Columbo?"

"Yeah. The TV detective."

"Jeez, how old *are* you, anyway? That show was on when I was a kid!"

She ignored my attempt at sarcasm. "Columbo would start to leave and then he'd come back and say he had *just one more question.*"

"And you think Agent Keglar might do that?"

"Maybe. He's old enough to have seen the show, isn't he?"

"You're even more paranoid than I am," I said.

"You think what's been happening to us is *paranoia*?"

I didn't really have to think about that. "No, I guess not."

"No, I guess not," she repeated, and this time it was her turn to be sarcastic.

"I don't think he'll be coming back – at least, I hope not. It's a long way up to Bay County. Like, at least 10 hours in good weather. And this is *not* good weather. He probably wanted to get started sooner than he did, too, but you kept asking him questions and then challenging his answers."

Teresa chuckled. "Yeah, that was fun."

"He did a pretty good job of keeping his cool, though."

"He was okay. I thought he was starting to lose it – starting to get a bit ticked off – toward the end."

"Maybe." I shrugged and got up to refill my coffee mug.

"What do you think he's going to do up there, anyway?"

"I don't know. Probably snoop around, bother the local cops, try to find out what happened to Danny. How his death up there connects with what's been happening down here."

Teresa took a giant swig of her coffee, finishing it, then got up and placed her mug in the sink. "I hope he figures something out," she said over her shoulder as she rinsed out the mug. She dried her hands and turned around. "Anyway, I've got to go call my insurance company about the house."

"Ooh, fun, fun, fun," I said.

She stuck out her tongue at me and disappeared into the bedroom to make the call.

While Teresa made her call, I started setting up my computer and printer on the kitchen table, getting ready to do a little decoding. I had to admit, she was taking this whole *someone-blew-up-my-house* thing a lot better than I would have. I'm pretty sure I would have been a lot more upset if that had happened to me. And, of course, spending time on the phone with an insurance agent always held the possibility of ruining one's outlook on the day.

But Teresa was still her usual, cheerful self when she returned from the bedroom. "Getting ready to go to work, I see," she said.

"Just setting stuff up," I said. "Everything go all right with your insurance claim?"

"Yeah. They're gonna send a guy out tomorrow to look at the house and assess the damage."

"You have to be there?"

"No. I called Natsuko. She has keys to my place and she's going to let him in."

"Natsuko?"

"My neighbor. The one who's teaching me to make Japanese food. Like yakimeshi. Remember?"

"Oh, yeah. Yakimeshi."

"So ... shall we start?"

"I guess so," I said.

I made a new pot of coffee and we went back to work decoding the first of the notebooks, using the same method we'd used for the first four pages. I read out one letter at a time and Teresa looked up the corresponding code letter and wrote it down. Then, once we had a paragraph, we divided the run-on letters into words. It was slow, hard work, but the results we got – the decrypted pages – grew increasingly more fascinating.

"This is getting pretty interesting," I said.

"Yeah. But it's taking us forever. It's going to take weeks to finish decoding all this stuff," was Teresa's reply.

She was right. Decoding the information in the notebook was slow work. But we kept at it, translating page after page into understandable English and adding them to our gradually-thickening stack of deciphered information. It became our job – get up in the morning, make coffee and spend the next 12 or 14 hours working on the notebooks.

The work on Teresa's place became a bit of a distraction, forcing her to make an occasional trip to Bartow to confer with carpenters, appliance installers and the like. I stayed at home, continuing to work on the notebooks and, perhaps more importantly, to act as a discouragement to anyone who might be planning an illegal entry into my house.

At some point – I think it was on the fourth day of our endeavor but, since what we did every day was practically identical to what we did the day before and the day after, I can't be sure – Teresa had what turned out to be both a good idea and a bad idea. "You know those flash drives I bought for you at Walmart?" she said.

"Yeah. What about them?"

"What were you going to do with them?"

"Make copies of all this, I guess." With a sweep of my arm, I indicated the kitchen table, stacked high with scratch paper, translations in progress, my laptop, printer, and Teresa's new computer, purchased from Walmart during one of her runs up to Bartow. Because of the more-or-less permanent clutter, the table was no longer suitable for eating, so all of our recent meals had been eaten in the living room.

"And then?"

"I don't know. I hadn't thought that far ahead. Hide them, I guess. Or give them to someone for safekeeping. You know, in case ours got stolen again."

"You should do that," Teresa said.

"Which one?"

"Give them to someone."

"Yeah, I should. I kinda forgot about that. Actually, we *both* should do it."

"Yeah, okay. I think that's a good idea. Who you gonna give yours to?"

"I dunno. The only person around here I'd trust with information like this is you."

She laughed. "Thanks for the vote of confidence, but I don't think that'll work."

"I know. Maybe I'll just send a copy of everything to my son in California. And I've got some cousins up in New England. I could send copies to them."

"Sounds good," she said.

"How about you?"

"Well, I was thinking I could give a copy to Natsuko. But then I thought, I don't really know her *that* well. And I wouldn't want her to get involved in all this – you know, end up with *her* house getting blown up or something."

"Yeah. So?"

"Uncle Bill, maybe? Or my sister, Julia, up in North Carolina."

"Let's do it," I said.

We took a break from our deciphering to make copies of the notebooks and the key. Mine were for my son, Ted, a carpenter out in Tuolumne, California – a town even smaller than Fort Meade – and for my cousin, Ann, in Laconia, New Hampshire. Teresa decided to send hers to her Uncle Bill and the aforementioned sister.

"In the morning, I'll take these into town and mail them," I told Teresa.

"Tomorrow's Sunday."

"Really? I thought it was Wednesday. Or maybe Thursday."

"Nope. Sunday," she said, giving me the kind of patient smile one normally reserves for small children who ask too many questions. Still, it was a very attractive smile.

That's one of the things I've always liked about Teresa. Her smile, I mean – not the fact that she can keep track of the days of the week. She really has a nice, friendly smile that lights up her entire face.

"So, today's Saturday, huh?" I said, without a trace of embarrassment. "Who knew? Okay, I'll mail them on Monday, then."

She smiled again.

Chapter 18 – Intrusion

Not much had happened to us since Special Agent Keglar's visit. There had been no break-ins, no visits from the police, no mysterious car doors slamming shut down the street in the middle of the night. There was one unnerving incident that took place around 3 A.M., a couple of nights ago – a helicopter flew low over my house and shined its searchlights down into the yard, waking both of us. But, as we watched from my kitchen window, it continued on down the street, beaming it's lights into yards on both sides of the street, so I guess it was a sheriff's helicopter, searching for someone. Perhaps Fort Meade had suffered another bicycle theft.

We decided to take a break from our labors on Sunday. Teresa made breakfast – French toast, eggs and ham – and we ate in the living room. The kitchen table had long ago surrendered to the clutter we called our workplace and no longer tolerated our presence unless we were working on decoding the notebooks.

In the afternoon, we watched TV. I'm a channel flipper, constantly switching from one channel to another, which drives Teresa bonkers. So I put her in charge of the remote for the afternoon.

We ended up watching golf. It was interesting, in a low-key sort of way. I've never paid much attention to the game but I suppose, now that I'm approaching retirement, I should get a head start and learn how to play. I've heard it's a requirement – even a law in parts of the state – that if you want to retire in Florida, you have to play golf.

By the time we'd had dinner and watched more TV, I was ready for bed. It had been a tough day, sitting around watching TV and doing ... well, nothing. So when the 11 o'clock news came on, I said goodnight to Teresa and excused myself to get ready.

I was beginning to relax a bit. Most of the paranoid thoughts that had dogged me earlier had faded away, probably because nothing unusual had happened to us in the past few days. Not since Special

Agent Keglar's visit, in fact. That he might have had something to do with our recent peaceful days briefly crossed my mind, then just as quickly faded away. I was tired and now that it appeared the government had lost interest in tormenting us, I was looking forward to a restful night, devoid of worries about aliens, FBI agents, and encoded notebooks.

Which is why it was a little surprising when, shortly after I'd fallen asleep, an alien tried to break in through my bedroom window. How did I know it was an alien? Because he made a noise as he was crawling through the window, which was open and directly behind the head of my bed. The noise woke me and, still half asleep, I reached up with my left arm, not really expecting to find anything there.

But I did. Find something there, I mean. Actually, I latched onto it. It was an arm – a cold, clammy, alien arm, and I had a firm hold of it with my left hand. Instantly, I was shocked into full wakefulness and I did what any self-respecting science fiction writer would have done under similar circumstances. I screamed – a long and loud AAARRGH!

We started to wrestle, arm against arm. And I was winning, even though I'm right-handed and was being forced to defend myself with my left hand. *Where the hell WAS my right hand, anyway?* Despite apparently being in control of the situation – this alien seemed incredibly weak – I let out another scream, just for good measure. (And don't mock me. If you woke up in a dark room and ended up wrestling with an alien, you'd scream, too!)

My screams brought Teresa, who was getting ready for bed, rushing into the room. "What's going on?" she said, turning on the light and temporarily blinding me.

"Help me!" I cried. "Hit him!"

"Hit who?"

"The alien!"

"Okay." She grabbed my pillow and used it to whack me in the head. "I got him," she said, and started to laugh.

"What the – ?" I sat up. My left hand had a firm grip on my cold, numb, lifeless right arm. I looked around. No alien. No *anybody*, other than Teresa. Just me, heart pounding, sitting on the bed with my right hand and arm firmly under the control of my left hand.

"Way to go," she said, still laughing. "Now that we've got him, what are we going to do with him?"

I swung my legs over the side of the bed and released my right arm from my left hand's vise-like grip, shaking it in an attempt to restore circulation. "What the hell just happened?" I said.

"An excellent question. I was just wondering that, myself."

Over cookies and milk in the living room, we sorted it out. Evidently, I had fallen asleep with my right arm under my body, causing it to go numb. And cold. The noise I heard that woke me was not someone at my window but just me turning over and flipping my right arm up behind my head, where it hit the headboard. Of course, I didn't feel it because that whole arm was as dead as a stump – no feeling whatsoever.

And when I reached up and clasped onto my right arm with my left hand, and felt that cold, seemingly-disembodied appendage, I automatically assumed an alien was climbing in through my window. Most likely that was because aliens had been on my mind a lot lately. At least, these were the conclusions Teresa came up with. And I couldn't come up with a better explanation.

"It makes sense, I guess," I said. "And it does explain everything."

"Except the screaming." She flashed a wicked grin.

I ignored that. Both the comment and the grin.

"Occam's razor," she said.

"What?"

"Occam's razor. You know, the simplest explanation that covers everything is invariably the correct one."

"Whatever." I ate four more cookies, finished my milk, and put the dishes in the sink. "I'm going back to bed. See you in the morning." I headed down the hall.

"Good luck sleeping!" she called after me. "Don't forget to close your window!"

"I'm gonna close it *and* lock it!" I yelled back, eliciting one more chuckle from Teresa.

Chapter 19 – Bitsy

Monday morning dawned cold, wet, and windy – an overnight storm had blown in. Fortunately, I had taken Teresa's advice and closed my window, but rain drumming on the glass woke me at first light. Not that it made much difference. It had been an uneasy sleep, with me tossing and turning and frequently semi-waking to worry about minor concerns such as whether or not I'd locked the kitchen door and should I buy more cookies when I went into town to mail the flash drives.

I stayed in bed, trying unsuccessfully to get back to sleep, until I heard Teresa moving around in the kitchen and the smell of coffee drifted back to my room. The aroma of freshly-brewed coffee was all that was needed to destroy my fantasy of getting more sleep, so I got up and headed for the bathroom. By the time I joined Teresa in the kitchen, she was on her second cup and already working on the notebooks.

She greeted me with a grin. "How's the alien wrestler this morning?"

I ignored the question and looked at what she was doing. "Anything exciting?"

"Just getting started," she said. "You going to the post office?"

A peek out the window revealed that the rain was still coming down, but not as heavily as when it woke me up. "I guess I'll go later. It looks as if this storm is moving off."

"Let's keep chipping away, then." She indicated the strewn-about papers in front of her with a sweep of her hand.

I poured a cup of coffee and grabbed a package of Famous Amos Chocolate Chip Cookies – my favorite – out of my goodies closet, checking my supply as I did so. Oh, oh. Only one box left. Time to start thinking about restocking.

Teresa gave me a disapproving look when I set the cookies on the table. "Really? Cookies for breakfast?" she said. But when I slid the box over to her, she grabbed a handful, gave me a half-grin and said, "They are good, though."

We worked until noon, by which time the rain had stopped, so I decided to make my run to the post office. "You want anything in town?" I said. "I can get lunch."

She shook her head. "We've got stuff here. I'll make something."

"Okay. I'll be right back."

The driveway was a little on the muddy side as I made my way out to my car. I was just starting to back out when I noticed Bitsy's mail truck coming down the street, so I got out and went down to the end of my driveway to greet her as she drove up. Good timing was going to save me from a trip into town, all of three miles away.

Bitsy was a couple of years younger than me and had been working for the United States Post Office since ... well, to hear her tell it, since sometime around the end of the Civil War. Her real name was Brenda Demmings but everybody called her Bitsy, although I don't know why. The nickname 'Bitsy' would seem to indicate a small person, but Bitsy was anything but small. She was big, with a loud, brassy persona that fit perfectly with her bleached-blonde hair and preferred attire – cargo shorts and aloha shirts. Just about everyone who knew her described her as 'a really good person who'd give you the aloha shirt off her back.'

"Hey, hotshot. How ya doin'?" she said, as her truck pulled up to my mailbox.

"Pretty good, Bitsy. How about you?"

"Fine, fine. How's that new girlfriend of yours working out?" She fixed me with a grinning, lascivious look.

"Not my girlfriend. We're just friends."

"Sure, sure," she said, still grinning. "Just friends. Everybody needs a friend."

"That's true."

"You sellin' any books?"

Bitsy was one of the few people in Fort Meade who knew I was a writer. That wasn't too surprising – Bitsy knew pretty much everything about everyone in town. "Here and there," I replied.

"So, not so much, huh?"

"Yeah, it could always bc better."

"Well, keep pluggin' away," she said. "Who knows? Next one could be a smash, and then, BOOM!" She made a sweeping motion through the air with her hand.

"Boom? What's that mean?"

"You know, money. Money, money, money! And fame. And then you can get out of here, move to the city, have some fun."

"I like it here, actually."

She gave me her best *are-you-kidding?* look. "Wanna hear something funny?"

"Sure. I'm always up for a joke."

"Not that kind of funny." She paused, becoming serious. "I'm 57 years old and I've never been out of the state of Florida." A hint of sadness tinged her face.

"You're kidding!"

"Nope. Never been north of Gainesville. Went up there to scc a football game, once."

"Wow," was all I could think of to say.

"But I've been saving my money, ya know, and when I retire, I'm gonna move somewhere out of state. Some place where it snows. I've never seen snow."

I laughed. "Boy, are you gonna be disappointed! I've lived up north and, let me tell you, snow is highly overrated."

She laughed with me. "We'll see, we'll see. So, what can I do for you today? You can't be standing out here in the cold just to visit with me." Although the storm had moved on, it had left behind a cloudy, cool day – the word 'cool' being relative down here in Florida.

"Oh, yeah." I'd almost forgotten the envelopes I was holding. I handed them to Bitsy. "Can you mail these for me? Priority Mail?"

"Sure. But these'll go First Class, if you want. Save you a bundle."

"Priority's good."

"Okay. You want insurance?"

"No, I don't think so. You need some money?"

"Nah. I'll put the receipt in your mailbox tomorrow and you can just put the money in there and I'll pick it up next time."

"Sounds good."

"Put the money in an envelope," she said. "So the squirrels won't see it and steal it." She laughed and drove off, waving goodbye.

I waved back at her, then went inside, had some soup and a sandwich, and got back to work.

Chapter 20 – The Great Mail Robbery

It wasn't until the next day that we heard about Bitsy. We were sitting in the living room, eating lunch and watching the noon news from Tampa with the sound off. At least, that's what it appeared Teresa was doing. As for me, I was looking at the TV but my thoughts were far away.

What I was thinking about was the book – sure to be a best-seller – that I was slowly constructing in my mind. The story of how I received the notebooks in the mail and how, with the help of my friend, Teresa, we decoded them. Specifically, my thoughts were about when, exactly, to reveal the *very* interesting information the notebooks were disclosing. Should I do it as the information unfolded, a little at a time? Or maybe wait until the end of the book, and include all the information at once, as a sort-of appendix? I had just about decided the appendix method offered more opportunities for drama when I was jolted back to the present by a picture on my TV screen.

"Hey! Turn the sound on," I said.

Teresa turned the sound back on.

"Did you see that?"

"What?" she said.

"That picture. Back it up."

She hit the rewind button.

"Stop! Stop! Right there, see."

"Isn't that your mail lady?"

"Yeah, I think so. Look. She's wearing a post office uniform – I've never seen that before. But that's her. Bitsy. Turn up the sound and start it."

Teresa started the paused news program. "Her name is Bitsy?" she muttered under her breath.

The smooth voice of the Tampa Bay announcer resumed, only louder. *"And when we come back, a very strange story out of Polk County,"* he was saying. And there, on the screen, all smiles and sunshine, was a picture of my long-time mail carrier, Bitsy, flashing what looked like a Mr. Spock style, split-fingered Vulcan greeting.

Teresa skipped the recording forward but we were still in the middle of the first commercial. We waited patiently through a succession of automobile ads, insurance offers, home security services, and finally, a Spanish language course that guaranteed you'd be speaking like a native in only 14 days. Teresa laughed at the claim and said, "Yeah, a native who only knows about a dozen words."

"Shh," I said, as the news resumed.

"And now, that story I was telling you about earlier," said Mr. Smooth Talker, the announcer. *"This is an absolutely amazing story out of Fort Meade. For the latest update, let's go to our Polk County reporter, Casper Wyoming."*

Teresa and I started laughing at the same time. "Did you hear that?" she said. "Is that his real name? Casper Wyoming?"

"Who knows?" I said, followed by, "Shhh!"

She punched me in the arm, still giggling. "That can't be real," she whispered.

The scene on the TV switched from from Mr. Smooth Talker to the front steps of the Fort Meade City Hall, where a tall, blonde, handsome young man – presumably the previously-mentioned Casper Wyoming – stood holding a microphone next to a smiling Brenda 'Bitsy' Demmings. Right on cue, he turned to the camera, smiled, and said, *"I'm here in the picturesque City of Fort Meade, down on the southern border of Polk County, speaking with local mail carrier, Mrs. Arthur Demmings, who had –"*

Bitsy reached over and grabbed Casper's hand – the one holding the microphone – and pulled it close to her. "Call me Bitsy, Cas, honey," she said, as if they were old friends. "Everyone calls me Bitsy."

"All right," said a smiling, slightly-surprised Casper. *"Bitsy it is."* He seemed to find Bitsy's nickname amusing, although I couldn't think of

any reason why a guy named Casper Wyoming would find humor in another's name.

"So, Bitsy," he continued, *"tell us what happened to you yesterday afternoon."*

"Sure, Cas. Be happy to." Bitsy grabbed the mic out of Casper's hand and, before he had a chance to protest, stepped forward, ready to tell her story. Teresa and I leaned forward in anticipation and Teresa turned the volume up even higher.

"Well, I was doing my route, heading out 98 towards Frostproof, musta been about 2:30 in the afternoon, when this big black car forces me off the road by cutting in front of me and stopping. Good thing I was going slow or I woulda run right into it."

Casper said, *"Uh-huh. Go on,"* and leaned over to try to retrieve his microphone, but Bitsy turned her back and continued with her story.

"So, these two big guys all dressed in black get out of the car and they run back to my truck and grab me – ya know, if I hadn'ta been so surprised, I'da popped one of 'em. Right in the mouth. But I didn't know what was going on."

A hand reached into the scene from off-screen and handed a second microphone to Casper, who appeared happy to get it. Or maybe relieved. *"All right. So what happened next?"* he said into his new mic.

"Well, one of these two guys – the bigger one – throws me in the back of the truck with the packages and stuff and then he pulls out this big hypodermic needle and he jabs me in the ass with it. Can ya say 'ass' on TV, Cas?"

"I think you just did, Bitsy," said Casper, looking slightly embarrassed.

I poked Teresa in the arm, causing her to look at me. "Needle in the butt – sound familiar?" I said.

"*Very* familiar," she replied.

Bitsy went on with her tale. "So, after he sticks me with the needle, he climbs on top of me and just sits there. Like he's waiting for the stuff in the needle to go to work, ya know – to put me to sleep."

"And did you, Bitsy? Did you go to sleep?"

"Yeah, eventually. But I was still awake when the other guy moved my truck. There was this side road, just a dirt road that went ... well, I don't know where it went, but they moved my truck a little ways down that road and then he – the other guy, not the guy sitting on me 'cause he couldn't do it 'cause I was still awake – went back and got the car."

"I see. And is that when it happened? Is that when you saw the ... you know, the thing?"

"Yeah, when they were moving the car. That's when I saw him. I'm not making this up, ya know – I really did see him."

Casper Wyoming turned away from his conversation with Bitsy and addressed us directly as the camera moved in for a close-up of his smiling face. *"And this is where the story gets really interesting. This was not your typical robbery. Was it, Bitsy?"* He turned his attention back to her. *"Tell us what you saw."*

"Well, I was starting to get a little sleepy by this time, ya know. But when that other guy was moving the car, I saw him. He was sitting in the back seat, just looking at us."

"And just who was this person in the back seat?"

"The alien."

"The alien?"

"Yeah. One of them little gray things with the big black eyes. But kinda on the fat side, ya know. And he was just sitting there, watching what was going on."

"So, we're talking about an extraterrestrial being here, right? Not someone from a foreign country?"

Bitsy turned to Casper and fixed him with an exaggerated look of surprise. "What country has people who look like that, Cas? This guy wasn't from a foreign country, he was from some other planet!"

"I see. An E.T. Are you sure that's what you saw, Bitsy? You said you were getting sleepy. Maybe you, uh, . . ."

"I wasn't *that* sleepy. At least, not yet."

"All right. So you saw the alien sitting in the car. Then what happened?"

"Well, I'm not entirely sure what happened next, Cas, 'cause right after that I did fall asleep. And when I woke up, my supervisor was there, and the sheriff, and a couple of EMTs, but the two guys and the alien were gone, of course. Apparently people had started calling up and complaining they hadn't got their mail, so my supervisor went out looking for me"

"But you were still in your truck, right?"

"Yeah, in the back. Where the packages and stuff go."

"And you were OK? No harm done? No lasting side effects or anything like that?"

"Nope. I'm fine."

Casper turned to the camera again. *"So. There you have it, folks. A mail robbery in the peaceful little town of Fort Meade, a place where crime of any kind is highly unusual."*

"We're not a town, we're a city," Bitsy corrected him. "We're the oldest city in Polk County. Been around since 1849, before the Civil War."

"I'm sorry, Bitsy. In the <u>city</u> of Fort Meade. A robbery, but not just a typical robbery. This one included an outer-space alien and the theft of a whole truckload of mail."

"That's not right. They didn't take all the mail."

Casper Wyoming's face registered surprise. *"No? They didn't steal the mail? I was told by the sheriff that this was a mail theft."*

"Yeah, it was. But they didn't take it all. They only took the outgoing mail. Just letters that I'd picked up earlier in my route. As far as I know, they didn't take any of the mail I was in the process of delivering. That's strange, too."

"Really? Well, that's a pretty unusual robbery, now in two ways. Aliens and very picky robbers, apparently."

"The cops'll get 'em," Bitsy said.

"I have no doubt," said Casper. He turned once again to the camera. *"So, crime comes to a small … city in Polk County, and it's a highly unusual crime, at that, involving as it does an outer-space alien, an E.T. But the authorities are on the case. There's talk the FBI will be getting involved, since the post office is a branch of the U.S. Government and mail theft is a federal crime. And I want to thank Mrs. Demmings, here, – "*

"It's Bitsy," said Bitsy, leaning into the shot.

"Yes. Bitsy. I want to thank her for sharing her story with us. We're certainly glad she's all right and is suffering no lasting effects from her harrowing experience – thank you, Bitsy. And now, back to Miki and Paul in the studio," said Casper. There was a final shot of the two of them standing there on the steps of City Hall, with Bitsy waving goodbye while Casper Wyoming smiled patiently, waiting for the cameraman to tell him they were done.

Teresa turned off the TV and looked at me. "Wow. Exactly like what happened to me. And that outgoing mail they stole – that had our flash drives in it."

"Yeah. I thought they were finished messing with us, but I guess not. It looks as if the game is back on."

Chapter 21 – Back to Work

The theft of mail from Bitsy's truck lent a new urgency to our decoding efforts and we returned to work with renewed energy and enthusiasm, determined to slog our way through the rest of dead Jimmy's notebooks as quickly as possible. Our resolution lasted for about two hours.

"A lot of this is really boring, don't you think?" Teresa said, leaning back and stretching.

"Yeah," I agreed. "But the interesting parts are really, *really* interesting. And I can see now why the government doesn't want its citizens to know about this, what's actually going on."

"You think if they find out, it will, you know, disrupt society, cause mass suicides, that kind of stuff? That's what they say."

I tried to look thoughtful. "I doubt it. I'm not planning on killing myself. How about you?"

"Not just yet," she said, smiling. "But we still have a lot of material to cover."

"So? Maybe later, then?"

She stuck her tongue out at me and attempted to punch me in the arm but missed.

"You're getting slow in your old age," I told her.

She tried again, leaning forward to get a better angle, and this time she connected.

"Ow!" I said, and we both laughed.

I was really enjoying having Teresa around. Her sunny disposition made a daunting task – turning dead Jimmy's encoded notebooks into readable material – almost enjoyable. And there were other benefits, too. Like getting some real, home-cooked food, for a change. Teresa was an excellent cook.

"What are we going to do about the flash drives?" she said.

"Whaddaya mean?"

"You know. The ones we mailed out. They're the reason Bitsy got robbed, right?"

"Yeah. I can't see any other reason why they'd take just the outgoing mail. If they were real thieves, they'd have taken everything. Maybe even the truck. Anyway, I've still got two left. I'll make copies and you can send one to your uncle or your sister and I'll send the other one to my son. And then I'll take them into town and mail them at the post office. That way we won't have to worry about Bitsy getting attacked again."

"Actually, I've got a better idea. I have to go meet with the carpenters tomorrow, and then I've got to go into work. I was thinking I could just give them to Judy and have her send them out with the company mail. No one would even know. Except Judy, of course."

"Judy being ... what? The mail clerk?"

"Yeah. Among other things."

"You're not going back to work tomorrow, though, are you?"

"No, I don't go back until next Monday – I told you this, already. But my paycheck is sitting up there waiting for me, so I thought I'd go pick it up and put it in the bank. Then maybe do a little shopping."

"Your boss is a great guy, giving you all this time off and still paying you. He *is* still paying you, right?"

"He is. Both a great guy and still paying me. At least, I *think* he's still paying me.. I'll find out for sure when I see the check."

"So, what time are you gonna go?"

"Early. I'm supposed to meet the carpenters at 8:30. Then after I get my check and deposit it, I'll stop at Publix or Walmart and pick up some groceries."

"Go to Publix. They have a better selection of cookies."

She punched me in the arm again. "You and your cookies," she said, laughing.

"And get some brownies, too."

She leaned back and gave me a studious look. "It's a miracle you don't weigh 400 pounds, the way you eat. How much *do* you weigh, anyway?"

"I dunno. About 160, usually."

"That's disgusting," she said, shaking her head.

"It's not my fault. My parents passed on good genes."

"Hey, listen, not to change the subject or anything, but what's the plan for all this stuff?"

"Plan? Stuff?"

"Yeah, the notebooks. After we finish decoding them, then what?"

"Good question." I paused to consider it, even though I knew what I was going to say. "Well, I've been thinking I'm gonna write a book."

"About the notebooks?"

"Yeah."

"You going to put all this new info in your book? This is a lot different than most of the theories I've heard about. And lemme tell you, I've heard *all* the theories."

I could believe that. As the self-described 'world's biggest science fiction fan,' Teresa was well-versed in the mythologies of alien encounters, UFO abductions, and the like. "I suppose I'll have to," I said. "At least, some of it. Otherwise, there's no reason to write the book."

"Yeah, that makes sense."

"You wanna be my co-writer?"

"What?"

"Be my co-writer. Help me write the book."

"Nope."

"Get your name on the cover and get paid half the royalties?"

"Not interested. I'm a reader, not a writer. I'll leave that up to you."

"Think about it," I said. "Teresa Ruiz, famous writer. You could introduce yourself to strangers like that. Or get business cards. *Teresa Ruiz, Author.*" I wrote her name in the air, using fancy script. "Your boss might even give you a raise, what with you being so famous and all."

"Yeah, right," she said. She paused, adopting a meditative air. "You know, I've been thinking."

"Uh-oh!"

"No, seriously."

"Okay, what? What have you been thinking?"

"Won't you get in trouble if you publish a book about this?"

"Why would I get in trouble?"

"Isn't all this stuff supposed to be secret? Classified?"

"I don't know. I didn't see any classification markings on the original notebooks, back when I had them. And the flash drives didn't have any, either."

Teresa looked doubtful. "Still, ..."

"Besides, I'm thinking the opposite will happen," I said. "Once I publish this and the information is out there, the government won't have any reason to mess with us, to be breaking into our houses and stealing our mail."

"Maybe. But they could still arrest you for disclosing classified secrets. Right?"

"Well, then, I'll publish it as a novel. And if they arrest me, I'll just say, *Hey! I made it all up. It's fiction, man! That's what I do. I'm a novelist – I write fiction!*" I stood up and assumed a dramatic pose, hands on hips, as I said the last part. I saw Superman use that pose, once. In a movie, of course.

Teresa laughed. "Very theatrical," she said. "You should be an actor."

"Maybe I will, someday," I said. "When I grow up."

She laughed again.

We spent the rest of the day as we did most every day, working on decoding the notebooks. It had become a grind – something we had to push ourselves to do. But we were slowly forcing our way forward and were nearly halfway through the second notebook.

Of course, it wasn't all work. We took frequent breaks – even going outside from time to time and walking around in the yard for a few minutes. And there were meals and the occasional TV show in the evenings. I usually made it a point to watch *Jeopardy* while Teresa fixed dinner. I had offered to help her several times but she always gave me the same answer – the best way I could help was by getting out of the kitchen and not bothering her.

The next morning – Wednesday – Teresa went up to Bartow to meet with the carpenters about the work on her house, and then to South Lakeland to pick up her paycheck, mail the flash drives, and do a little shopping. I stayed behind to work on the notebooks and, as she had put it, 'to guard the house.' Guarding the house was the easy part. Nothing unusual happened. Working on the notebooks, however, was far from easy. Without Teresa there to help me, the decoding process took three times as long.

Something else was also slowing me down. As we'd gotten deeper into the second notebook, I had begun to suffer from what I can only describe as *disappointment syndrome*. A great deal of the information in notebook 2 was similar, if not identical, to what had already been revealed in the first notebook. There were some new details but most of it was ... well, redundant. And while the first notebook had been full of spectacular and frequently-shocking new information, much of which Teresa and I had never heard before (and which I will reveal to you later in the book), notebook 2 tended to merely confirm what had been divulged in book 1.

So when Teresa returned at around noon, I was more than happy to take a break and help her put away the groceries. And my happiness wasn't just because those groceries contained a fresh supply of cookies, either. There was also a bucket of fried chicken!

Chapter 22 – Friends with Benefits

"I don't know whether I should tell you this or not," Teresa said.

"Tell me what?" I mumbled through a mouthful of chicken. We were sitting on the steps outside my kitchen, the bucket of chicken, two beers, and a roll of paper towels between us, chowing down. Once again our cluttered kitchen table had refused to allow us to use it for its intended purpose – eating. Moving all our junk and then putting it back after we ate was just too much trouble.

She pointed at a parked car about a block down the street. "See that green car?"

"Umm," I said. That meant yes.

"This morning, I thought maybe I was being followed on my way up to Bartow. By a green car."

"Really?" I said, suddenly more interested in Teresa's story than the chicken.

"Yeah. All the way from just outside of town, there was this green car several car-lengths behind me. When I changed lanes, it changed lanes. When I slowed down or speeded up, it did, too."

"So what happened when you got to Bartow?"

"Well, when I turned at East Main, it turned, too. But you know that little bend in the road, just past the railroad tracks? I went to the left and the green car went straight."

"It was probably a coincidence – just someone on their way to play golf." Bartow Golf Course is only three blocks from Teresa's house.

"Probably," she agreed, although the look on her face indicated she still had doubts.

"How's about I take a walk down there and check out the car as I walk by?"

"What good'll that do?"

"I dunno. Can't hurt. I can write down the license plate number, in case anything happens."

"What could happen?" she said, a faint hint of concern clouding her face.

"You know. In case you get followed again by a green car, you can pull over and force it to pass you, and then you can see if it's the same car."

"Oh. Okay. That sounds good. Go check it out."

I grabbed a couple of paper towels and degreased myself, then snatched a pencil and a paper scrap off the kitchen table and started down the driveway to check out the green car. But I didn't get far. As soon as I turned onto the sidewalk and headed toward where it was parked, it pulled out and drove away. Not by itself, of course – someone was behind the wheel. I just couldn't see who it was.

"That was a little weird," I told Teresa, after I'd rejoined her on the steps and helped myself to another piece of chicken.

"I agree," she said, staring down the street at the spot where the car had been parked. "Do you know who lives in that house? By the car?"

"Yeah. An old retired couple. The Mackenzies, or Macdougals – something like that. Mac-something. I don't really know them. Just enough to nod and say hi."

"Is their car green?"

"I think it's red. A red SUV. But that green car could have been a visitor."

"I suppose. But you have to admit, it *is* kinda odd."

"Yeah, well, just add it to the list of strange happenings around this place."

We finished the rest of our makeshift picnic, washed up and went back to work, putting thoughts of strange happenings temporarily out of mind. But later that evening, while we were getting ready for bed, we were again visited by a helicopter. This time the visit appeared to be solely for the purpose of annoying us, or perhaps intimidating us, because it hovered low over the house for a couple of minutes, shining its lights down into my yard and illuminating the interior of the house, before turning off the lights and moving away.

And then, at about 4 A.M., the helicopter returned. Or perhaps it was a different helicopter. Either way, it woke us up by going through the same routine as the earlier one – hovering low and shining lights into the house.

"What are they trying to do? Scare us?" Teresa said, joining me as I watched from the kitchen window.

"Maybe. Or maybe they're just trying to piss off my neighbors."

"I'll bet they're doing a good job of that."

"Yeah, I'll bet they are."

"I wonder what your neighbors think about all this, anyway – wonder if they've put it together. Made the connection, I mean. Helicopters buzzing the neighborhood at night, Bitsy getting robbed – you think they've noticed the weird things that have been happening around here lately?"

"I doubt it. Unless things are happening directly to you, you probably don't even notice."

"Or, maybe they *have* noticed, and their suspicions are growing. Maybe they've already decided you're a spy or a secret agent or something. Maybe they're even cooperating with the government."

This is the part where Teresa usually punches me in the arm to show me she's kidding, so I waited, expecting it. But this time she didn't, so I decided she was being serious. "Yeah, that's me. A regular James Bond," I said.

The helicopter eventually turned off its lights and flew off down the street, and we went back to bed. But if its intention had been to ruin our sleep, it had done a good job. At least, as far as I was concerned. I tossed and turned, unable to return to that desired state of reduced consciousness. Which is why I wasn't completely surprised when Teresa knocked softly on my bedroom door about 20 minutes later.

"Yeah, I'm awake," I replied.

The door opened and she stood there, hesitantly. She was wearing a sheer, nearly-transparent nightie – what they used to call a *baby doll* when I was younger but which probably has a cooler and more politically correct name these days – and the night-light in the hallway provided just enough light to make it appear invisible. She was, for all intents and purposes, standing there practically naked.

"Can't sleep?" I said, sitting up and taking a good look.

"Yeah."

"I like your outfit."

"Thanks."

"So, ...?"

"I was thinking ..." Her voice trailed away.

"Thinking what?"

"Can I sleep with you?"

I was a little surprised by her question, and there was a slight pause before I said, "Absolutely."

"You sure? You don't sound certain."

"But I am." I moved over to one side of the bed and pulled the covers back on the other side. "Hop in." I patted the open part of the bed with my hand.

She left the door partly open so that a little bit of light flowed into the room, crossed over to the bed and slipped in beside me. "Don't get any ideas," she said. "I'm just lonely. And a little anxious. So, one rule. No hanky-panky. Cuddling only. Okay?"

"Sure, a cuddling-only rule. That's works for me," I said, while at the same time thinking, *This is never gonna work!*

She turned her back to me and snuggled up close, so that we were in a *spooning* position. "That's nice," she mumbled into her pillow.

It *was* nice. But awkward, too. I wasn't sure what she was up to. Had she come in here to seduce me? Or was it simply what she'd said – she was lonely and anxious? And that's why she'd declared a cuddling-only rule? I decided to play it cool and let her take the lead.

A few minutes went by. I was just beginning to think she'd fallen asleep when she suddenly turned her head and said, "Something's poking me in the back. Is that you?"

"Sorry. I can't really help that."

She rolled over. "That's okay." She paused, studying my face in the dim light. "Wanna hear something funny?"

"What?"

"I lied to you before."

"About what?"

"About being lonely and anxious."

"You're not?"

"No."

"What are you, then?"

"Well, ..."

"Well, what? If you're not lonely and anxious, what are you?"

"Horny as hell," she said.

"What?"

"You heard me."

"Girls don't get horny," I said.

"Oh, yeah? What do they get, then?"

"Guys get horny, girls get *juicy*. I read it in a book, once."

She giggled, sat up and punched me in the shoulder. I knew one of those would be coming, eventually. "All right, then. Juicy. So ... ?" she said.

"Yes, indeedy. I think maybe I can help with that." I pulled her back down and kissed her. Teresa may have had a *cuddling-only* rule, and I may have agreed to abide by it, but you know what they say about rules – they were made to be broken.

Chapter 23 – A False Alarm

The smell of coffee woke me in the morning, about an hour later than usual. The bed next to me was empty – Teresa was gone. I could hear her, out in the kitchen, presumably making breakfast, as I tumbled out of bed and headed for the bathroom.

She was fully clothed in shorts and a T-shirt, rinsing a pan in the sink when I finally made it to the kitchen. I sneaked up behind her and kissed her on the cheek. "Good morning, beautiful," I said.

She smiled up at me. "Perfect timing. Look." She pointed at the kitchen table.

I looked. She had pushed our computers and papers down to one end of the table and, in their place were two plates of scrambled eggs – with onions, the way I like them – plus bacon, fried potatoes and toast. "Wow! I knew I smelled something good out here. Besides you, I mean."

She fake-punched me in the arm and grinned. "Lemme just pour some coffee and we're good to go."

"What's the occasion, anyway?" I said.

"Nothing special. I just got tired of those breakfast sandwiches you seem to like so much."

We took our time eating and it was almost 10 o'clock by the time we got to work. Twenty minutes in, Teresa's phone rang. She answered and went into the living room room to talk.

I could hear her end of the conversation. At least, part of it. I heard her say," What! Not again!" in a loud voice and then, "Yeah, okay. I'll be there in about a half-hour."

"That was quick," I told her when she came back to the kitchen.

"I've gotta go to Bartow," she said.

"What's up?"

"That was the police. Someone broke into my house."

"And, ... ?" I said.

"They got caught. The cops arrested them."

"That's great. What was that cop's name at your house? The one who was going to arrest us? Officer O'Brien? He told us they were keeping an eye on your house."

"Yeah. O'Brien."

"So why do you have to go to Bartow?"

"Whoever they arrested claims they have permission to be in my house. The cops want me to come up there and ID them in person."

"So who was it?"

"I don't know. They wouldn't tell me."

"You don't think it was – "

"Who?" she said.

"You know. Danny?"

"Danny's dead, dummy!"

"Wow. Nice alliteration. But dead Jimmy was dead for over 40 years – at least I thought he was – and then, bang! Suddenly he wasn't."

"I don't think this is like that. Though I wish it was." There was a sadness in her voice and I felt bad for making light of the whole *dead Danny* situation.

"Maybe it was your neighbor, Natsuko," I suggested.

"I doubt it. She has a key and I wrote her a note, giving her permission to be there."

"The cops probably think it's a forgery."

"Yeah, that could be. Anyway, I've gotta get going. The sooner I get there, the sooner I'll find out what's going on." She disappeared into her bedroom to change her clothes.

"You want me to go with you?" I called after her.

"Nope. I can handle this."

I cleaned up the kitchen, rinsing the plates and stacking them in the sink, while Teresa got ready. After she left, I pulled our computers and notes back into position and went to work. I was still at it when she returned, carrying a bag of groceries, shortly after noon.

"Just a couple of things I forgot yesterday," she explained, holding the bag aloft.

"So. What happened?" I said by way of greeting.

"Nothing. It was kind of a false alarm." She put the groceries in the fridge and flopped down into the chair across from me.

"You mean, nobody broke into your house?"

"They did. But it was just some neighborhood kids. Two 14-year-old boys and a 15-year-old girl. They were just ... exploring."

"Yeah, I'm sure that's all they were doing," I said. "How do you know they weren't a gang? Working for the government?"

She cast a disparaging glance in my direction. "The same way I know you're not *really* an idiot," she said.

"Oh," was all I could say to that.

"You shoulda been there – it was really interesting."

"How so?"

"Well, first of all, you remember Officer Sweeney?"

"You mean Sweetness?"

She smiled. "Yeah, him. He was running the show. And then there were the three kids, looking all scared and shame-faced, and their parents. Well, some of them anyway. Three dads and a mom. And they did not look like happy campers."

"Can't blame 'em, I guess. The parents, that is."

"Yeah, they definitely were pissed off. At least, at first."

"What's that mean? At first?" I got up to refill my coffee cup. "You want coffee?" I asked her.

"Second pot?"

"Yeah."

"Sure. Anyway, Officer Sweeney told me the kids claimed they had permission to be there. In the house. And he wanted to know if that was true."

"Was it?"

"Kind of. I never saw the girl before, but I caught the two boys in my back yard one morning. I'm pretty sure they were smoking a joint."

"Obviously, hardened criminals," I observed. "But why would they choose your yard to commit their dastardly deeds?"

She narrowed her eyes and stared across the table at me. "You've gotta stop talking like a 19th century mystery writer," she said. "Nobody says things like *dastardly deeds* anymore."

I chuckled. "Everybody's a critic. So what happened with the kids?"

"You know that empty lot behind my house? They were sitting on the ground, out by the hedge there, smoking. I guess they thought they were still in the vacant lot, but they weren't. They were in my yard."

"And? Did you rat them out?"

"Of course not. For smoking marijuana? Get real."

"It's still against the law here in Florida," I said.

"Laws, shmozz. I'm not gonna get two young kids a criminal record for smoking weed."

"So what did you do?"

"Nothing. They were all, like, guilty-looking and embarrassed and trying to hide what they were doing. And I told them to relax, it was okay that they were in my yard and I wasn't going to call the police or their parents or anything. And then I told them not to be late for school."

"What did they say to that?"

"They thanked me – many times. And then they informed me it was summertime and there was no school, and they were planning to go swimming. So I told them to watch out for alligators. They each gave me a funny look and then they left."

"And is that what you told Sweetness?"

"Not exactly. I forgot to mention the part about the marijuana. But I said that I caught them playing in my yard once and told them they were welcome to play there anytime, and even to come in the house if they wanted to."

"And he believed you?"

She gave a little face-shrug. "I doubt it. It's hard to tell from his face what he thinks. He always looks ... you know."

"Grumpy?" I suggested.

"Yeah. Anyway, with me saying they had permission to be there, no crime was committed, so they released the kids without charges. Officer Sweetness did not appear to be happy with that decision."

"But then, he never looks happy," I noted.

"You're right about that. But their parents sure looked relieved. The mom even whispered, *Thank you*, across the table to me. I'll bet they were already wondering how much a lawyer was gonna cost."

"Wow, you really are an old softy, aren't you?"

"Sometimes I am, sometimes I'm not. But today, for some reason, I just seem to be in a really good mood. Thanks to you." She leered at me from across the table.

"Me?" I said, feigning ignorance.

"Yeah, you. Yesterday, I probably would have told the cops to lock 'em up! But today, I feel so good I just couldn't do that. And I owe it all to *you*!" she said, and laughed.

This time it was *my* turn to punch to punch *her* in the arm. And I did so. Lightly, of course.

Chapter 24 – A Flickering Light

With Teresa's false alarm out of the way, we returned to our work. Things remained calm until Saturday – no hovering helicopters interrupted our sleep and no mysterious green cars were visible anywhere in the neighborhood. Teresa moved some of her things into my room and began sleeping with me each night, claiming the bed in her room was "lumpy" and that she was "lonely and afraid, sleeping all alone." Although I didn't believe either excuse, I was more than happy with our new arrangement.

So, things were progressing rather smoothly, for a change. We were well into the third notebook and could see, as the old cliché goes, "the light at the end of the tunnel." Hopefully, that light wouldn't turn out to be a train coming toward us.

And then, just as we were beginning to put any lingering paranoia out of our minds and enjoy our Saturday afternoon, a dark cloud from our recent past blew in and caused 'the light' to flicker. Our old friend, FBI Senior Special Agent Marvin Keglar, reappeared at my kitchen door.

I wasn't glad to see him and I wasn't as friendly this time around. "Oh, it's you," was my less-than-enthusiastic greeting when I opened the door and found him standing there, peering at me through my screen door. "What do you want?"

He ignored my lukewarm welcome. "Good afternoon, Mr. Novicki. You remember me, don't you? Senior Special Agent Keglar. We spoke the other day."

"Of course I remember you – I'm not senile."

"No, of course not. Please forgive the implication, I was just trying to be polite." He paused. "I was wondering if I might have a word or two with you."

"I don't think so."

"Pardon?"

"I don't want to talk to you." I glanced over at the table, where Teresa sat, surrounded by our computers and our notes – what would no doubt be described as *incriminating evidence* in a court of law. There was a slight panicky, *what-do-I-do?* look on her face as she observed our interaction.

"And why not?" Agent Keglar said, his face utterly devoid of emotion. No disappointment at my denial of his request. No surprise. Nothing. I couldn't help but think how professional he was – exactly what one would expect from an FBI agent. I'd be willing to bet he was a great poker player.

"I don't need a reason," I said. Which was true. You don't have to talk to the cops or the FBI just because they want to talk to you – you can always say no. But if you do agree to talk to them, you'd better tell the truth. Lying to them is a criminal offense.

"That's true," he said. "But it won't take long. It's just a couple of quick questions."

"That's what you said last time – just a couple of quick questions – and then you spent half a day here questioning us." This was a bit of an exaggeration but I'm sure he got the point.

"Well, I don't think it was quite that long," he said, attempting a smile. "And much of the reason for it taking so long was because your girlfriend – " He paused, apparently waiting for me to correct what he must have intended as a deliberate mischaracterization of our relationship, but I didn't, so he continued. "Because your girlfriend had more questions for me than I did for the two of you."

"Whatever," I said, keeping my expression neutral and my voice calm. I suspect I'd also make a pretty good poker player.

"Would you mind answering just one question, then?"

"Yes, I would mind. I don't want to talk to you and I want you to leave."

"So you're unwilling to cooperate in our investigation?"

"That's right. I don't think I know enough about this to want to cooperate. What is it that you're investigating, anyway? I never quite understood what it is you're trying to do."

"I think I explained this to you when I was here before. I'm looking into all the strange things that have been happening around you and Miss Ruiz – the break-ins, the explosion at her house in Bartow, the death of her ex-husband up in the panhandle, and now, the robbery of your letter carrier, Mrs. Demmings. I'm trying to figure out exactly how and *if* they're connected."

"Bitsy? What's that got to do with us?" I said. Of course, *I* knew how Bitsy's mail-truck robbery was connected to us, and so did Teresa. But how did Senior Special Agent Keglar know we were the reason she was robbed? Was he just fishing?

He smiled a *gotcha* smile. "Well, when I interviewed her, I asked her if anything odd had happened on her route that day."

"You mean, like getting run off the road and robbed?"

"In addition to that. And she said the only unusual thing that happened that day – other than the robbery – was that you were waiting for her out front when she arrived here, at your house, and you gave her four small, padded envelopes to mail."

"I was on my way to the post office and I saw her coming down the street, so I gave them to her to save myself a trip into town," I told him. As soon as I said it, I realized what he was doing. He'd smoothly conned me into talking to him.

"What was in the envelopes?"

This time it was my turn to smile. "As I explained earlier, I won't be answering any questions." I took a quick peek at Teresa, who looked a lot more relaxed than she had a couple of minutes earlier. She smiled at me and I winked back at her, first checking that Agent Keglar wasn't looking.

"That's really too bad, Mr. Novicki. I thought you were as interested in figuring all this out as I was."

Teresa suddenly popped out of her chair and joined us at the door. "Hello, Senior Special Agent Keglar. How nice to see you again."

He nodded. "Ah, Miss Ruiz, it's nice to see you, also."

"What brings you here today?" she said, as if she'd just arrived from a far-away room.

"Well, I had a couple of questions I was hoping your ... boyfriend might be willing to answer for me. But it seems he doesn't want to cooperate. Perhaps you can persuade him to change his mind?" He looked hopeful.

"I don't think so. I'm pretty sure we won't be answering any of your questions today." Her voice was friendly and she was smiling as she said it, which seemed to have a confusing effect on Agent Keglar.

"I'm sorry. What?" he said.

"No answers for you here, I'm afraid. But I do have a question for you."

"Of course you do," he said.

"I thought I heard my boyfriend ask you to leave. And yet, you're still here. Why?"

Hey! How about that? She called me her 'boyfriend.' Does that mean we're a couple again?

Obviously, this was not the question Agent Keglar was expecting. He looked even more confused than he had a moment earlier. Confused *and* disappointed. I began to suspect I was wrong about his chances at the poker table.

"So. No help from you, either?" he said.

"I'm afraid not," she said, still friendly-like and smiling.

"You know, I didn't want to have to resort to this, but I can always get a warrant and come back."

"What good will that do? We still don't have to talk to you."

"No. But it will allow me to search the premises."

"For what?" she said. "You can't search the house based on some vague investigation you say you're conducting. You have to be looking for something specific. And you have to list it on the search warrant. So what are you searching for? What do you hope to find?"

Wow! I was impressed. Teresa was, as they say, *sticking it to the man!* I guess I shouldn't have been that surprised, though. In addition to being the world's biggest science fiction fan, Teresa also liked to read mysteries and true-life crime novels. And evidently she'd learned quite a bit from her reading.

Senior Special Agent Keglar ignored her question and turned to leave. But as he started down the steps he turned back to us and said, "I'll be back with that warrant. In the meantime, I'd advise you not to leave town."

"I have to go back to work on Monday," Teresa said. "In Lakeland."

"Then don't leave the county." He turned, went down the steps and walked across to where his car was parked.

"Don't forget to have a judge sign it," Teresa called to him as he was getting into his car. "Search warrants aren't any good without a judge's signature. A *real* judge!"

He waved a hand without looking our way, got in his car and backed out of the driveway.

"Do you think he'll come back?" she said, as we stood at the door, watching him leave.

"I don't think so. He was probably bluffing. Anyway, today's Saturday. He'll have a hard time finding a judge."

"If he does come back, make sure you read the search warrant. They have to show it to you – it's the law. I've read that sometimes they fool people. They just wave a fake warrant and march right into the place."

"Yeah, I've heard that."

"That's kinda interesting, too."

"What? What's interesting?"

"That." She pointed down the street just as Agent Keglar's car rounded a bend and disappeared from view. "His car," she said. "It's green."

Chapter 25 – Closure

Teresa went back to work on Monday, leaving me to muddle through the notebooks by myself. Agent Keglar hadn't come back, which was one of the few good pieces of news that had come our way recently. Hopefully, his threat of returning with a search warrant was only bluster and he'd leave us alone for the foreseeable future.

When Teresa came home from her job each evening – usually about five – she was seldom in the mood to get right to work, so I'd take a break from my decoding and we'd relax in the living room with a couple of beers while we discussed the events of the day and how much progress I'd made. By the time we'd had dinner and begun work, it was typically almost nine o'clock. And, since we usually knocked off at about 11 to watch the late news, we didn't get much done in the evenings.

At this stage of our work – almost finished – we really had to push ourselves to complete what we'd started. We weren't getting much new information. Most of what we were now decoding – notebook #3 – was merely confirmation of earlier revelations. To tell the truth, that wasn't anywhere near as much fun as finding out the meaning of existence, where the little grays were from, and what happens when you die had been. But every once in a while, a new tidbit would pop up, and it was just enough to keep us going.

One big worry floated almost continuously through my mind, although I didn't mention it to Teresa. It was that, just as we finished decoding the three notebooks and had all this interesting new knowledge to share with the world, we'd be arrested or otherwise detained. And in the process, all our hard work would magically disappear, never to be seen again. Maybe Teresa and I would also *magically disappear.*

Of course, there were the flash drives we'd sent to my son and to Teresa's uncle. That's assuming they got them – we hadn't heard anything, yet. But then, it had only been three days since Teresa gave them to Judy, the mail clerk, to mail.

Even if the flash drives eventually did get delivered, our relatives had no idea what they contained because we hadn't told them. We'd just asked them to 'hang onto them for us.' Plus, the versions we'd sent to them were still encrypted. Anyone looking at the files would have no idea of the meaning of the jumble of letters they were seeing. So, if anything happened to Teresa and myself, it would be unlikely that the information from dead Jimmy's notebooks would ever see the light of day.

I was determined not to let that happen. And the way to do it, I was convinced, was to write a book and publish it. Even if I ended up in prison for disclosing classified government information, at least the knowledge would be out there for people to see and there would be little the government could do about it. As my dear, sweet, departed mother used to say, *once the cat is out of the bag, you really need to buy more kitty litter!* Or something like that.

There were other worries, too, although they were less specific. General anxiety would be a good way to describe how I felt. But the thoughts that ran through my head were worrisome enough to cause me to lose sleep and I spent a couple of nights tossing and turning in my recliner, not wanting to wake Teresa by doing the same thing in our bed.

A few years earlier, my son had sent me an NRA sticker. A big, round decal, actually, with a bald eagle flying through the air carrying crossed rifles and the words *National Rifle Association* around the edge. He'd meant it as a joke – I don't own a gun and I'm not really the type who joins national organizations. But now I dug it out of the drawer I'd tossed it in and plastered it onto the window of my kitchen door, at eye level. Just to give any potential intruders something to think about, you know?

I also put my imaginary dog's food and water dishes where they were a bit more conspicuous – like, a foot from the door – and filled the water dish with water. Although I realized the chances of all this subterfuge actually fooling anyone were slim, it made me feel better. By the way, the name on the dog dish – *Godzilla*!

And so, slowly, despite all the interruptions and attempts to intimidate us that had happened along the way, we found ourselves nearing the end of notebook #3. One day – it must have been on a weekend because Teresa was here – she leaned back, stretched and said, "That's it."

"It?" I said.

"Yeah. That's the end of it. We're finished."

"Great." I leaned back and folded my hands on my stomach.

"You're kidding! Great? That's all you can say after weeks of working on this?"

I shrugged. "*Really* great?"

"I'm disappointed. I thought you'd be happy we were finished."

"I *am* happy," I said, and that was true. But there was an anti-climactic feeling laying on top of my happiness, pushing it down and adding a layer of disappointment to it. So much of what had happened over the past few weeks remained a mystery.

"You want a beer?" she said. "To celebrate the end of our work?"

"Sure. Why not? But we're not really finished, you know. *Your* work is finished, but I still have plenty to do."

She laughed and punched me in the arm. "Not my problem. As long as *I'm* finished, I'm happy and ready to celebrate."

I wish I could say our story came to an exciting conclusion, a grand denouement that revealed exactly what was going on. It would have been nice to know for sure who was behind our occasional harassment, what was the point of letting Teresa and Bitsy get a glimpse of a fake alien, and why Danny had to die. But alas, that wasn't to be. Strange things just ... stopped happening. Low-flying helicopters no longer buzzed my house. Green cars were nowhere to be seen as Teresa drove back and forth to work. Our lives took on a semblance of normalcy.

Of course, now that the decoding was done, there was the book to write. I needed to get the jumble of thoughts that was tumbling through my mind organized and down onto paper. Actually, onto a computer, but you know what I mean.

And so, part one of this book – the backstory – comes to an end. All that remains is for me to organize, condense, and write down *the important parts* of the 20 years worth of information supplied to dead Jimmy by the three aliens. Easy, right? So let's get to it and see what they had to say.

PART II - DISCLOSURES

As you might imagine, dead Jimmy's notebooks contained a *lot* of information. About a *lot* of different subjects. I could probably write two or three books based on what I learned from them. But I'm not going to – at least, not right away, anyway.

What I *am* going to do is offer up a condensed version of what I consider to be the more important information in the notebooks. There are several reasons for deciding to do it this way, not the least of which is the desire to get these details before the public's eyes as soon as possible, in order to protect ourselves. Both Teresa and I believe that once this knowledge is made public, the harassment and attacks against us will stop for good. I hope we're right.

Another reason for doing it this way is that all three aliens tell, for the most part, identical stories. Although dead Jimmy spent years with each alien, at separate times throughout his military career, each alien provided remarkably similar information. To combat the redundancy, information is presented as though it came from only one alien entity.

Some very minor differences in the aliens' stories did exist, however, and a few of these are mentioned. In addition, all of this information comes with several caveats, both from dead Jimmy and from Teresa and me. Jimmy, for example, mentions that he has no way of knowing if what the aliens are telling him is true. They could all have been programmed to tell the same story if they were caught. Or maybe, because they were all telepathically connected, once one of them told their captors a story, the rest all knew about it.

Jimmy also expressed concerns over his abilities as an alien translator. After all, it's not as if words were involved. An alien would telepathically implant an image into Jimmy's mind and it would be up to him to figure out what it meant. An example he mentions is that all three aliens showed him images of uninhabitable, abandoned coastal cities around the world due to rising sea levels. But was it a vision of the future of Earth, or was it a warning? Jimmy didn't know.

Caveats from me and Teresa include the fact that until dead Jimmy reached out to me, I hadn't heard from him in over 40 years. I believed he was dead. For all we know, he could have contacted me from a mental hospital somewhere near Chicago, where he'd spent the past 40 years compiling notebooks based on fantasies and hallucinations. We cannot prove *any* of the information contained in dead Jimmy's notebooks, but we believe it's real. If not, why were we harassed and attacked?

With these warnings in place, I'll proceed. Much of this information is considerably different than what you might have learned in school, or in church, or along the road of life. Some of it is also upsetting – especially is you're a religious person – so if you *do* get upset by what's revealed, remember that little gray aliens, captured by humans, may well be programmed to lie, and dead Jimmy could be a liar, as well. Or just insane.

So, let's see what little gray aliens have to say about the meaning of life, what happens when you die, and just what's going on here on this crazy, mixed-up planet called Earth.

* * * * *

The Meaning of Existence

The notebooks contain more information about this than any other subject. This may be because of a strong interest in the subject on Jimmy's part, although I'm not sure. But I do suspect it, not only for this subject, but for everything the aliens discussed with Jimmy. It seems they talked about what Jimmy was interested in, not what was on the aliens' minds. Of course, this might be because Jimmy was given a script to follow by higher-ups. Also, it's important to keep in mind that the aliens were prisoners and dead Jimmy was, for want of a better word, their interrogator.

So, here goes. All three aliens agreed that this life we lead, here on planet Earth, has no great, mystical meaning, but is merely a game. Nothing, according to them, is real – we live in an artificial, projected universe, full of illusions and hallucinations. And they provided plenty of what they called *evidence* for their claims.

The whole concept is extremely complicated, but I'll do my best to explain it. It goes like this. The current game has been around for about 500 years, roughly from the time when Columbus discovered America. But before this current game, there were other, smaller games – hundreds of them – upon which the present-day game is based. (These other, smaller games still exist, apparently, but, with the exception of the Ancient Egypt game, they're no longer popular.)

Among these earlier games were a European game, an African game, an Asian game, an American game, and so on. And there were subsets of each of these games. For example, one could play the American game, which included North, Central, and South America up until the time the white Europeans came, or one could play a smaller subset that included just, say, what is now the American Southwest or one that encompassed only the Amazon region. The Asian game also included numerous subsets, including ones for Japan, Thailand, India, and several others. In some cases there was overlap between games and/ or game subsets – European players could visit China, for example, but not Japan.

And so, sometime about 500 years ago, many of these smaller games were joined together to produce this one big game we are all now playing. Although it's never made *completely* clear, it appears the reason for the continually-increasing sizes of the games has something to do with increased computing power – none of the games, including this one we're in now, are controlled by gods with magical powers. Science rules, not magic.

The one thing all the games, including the current one, have in common is that they are based on conflict. While a nice, peaceful existence might seem like what most people want, that would only lead to boredom. Wars, violence, anger and the like are what actually make a game interesting. To ensure conflict, the creators infused each game with multiple languages, multiple religions, multiple cultural beliefs, and the built-in belief of each player that *my way is the best way.*

You can see the results of this by looking at any history book. Our history – which includes the histories of the current game in which we're all now involved (since about the time of Columbus) and those of earlier games which were carried over into this game – is one of constant wars, battles, skirmishes, coups, and assassinations. In other words, conflict. Despite the fact that religious people constantly pray for peace, we never get peace. We get more conflict. Because that's the way the game is designed and played – *conflict* makes it work.

A major component of the game is the idea of *red herrings*. If you're unfamiliar with the term, I think the best definition of a red herring is that it's a *fake clue*. It's the reason the detective in a murder mystery can figure out who the murderer is but you can't – the writer of the mystery has sprinkled the tale with clues as to the identity of the killer, but some of the clues are real and some are fake. The detective in this tale knows the difference – which clues are real and which are fake, or *red herrings*, which makes it easy for him or her to identify the culprit and difficult for you.

According to all three aliens, our reality is full of these fake clues. And while the purpose of a red herring in a mystery is to confuse the reader as to the killer's identity, its purpose in our game is slightly different – it's to confuse us about what's really going on. Red herrings are scattered throughout our game to prevent us from realizing we're playing a game.

You may not have noticed that the history of the human race is constantly changing, because it's been happening gradually. But, as archaeologists and historians make new discoveries, they are forced to make adjustments to their – and *our* – beliefs. We now believe that the human race has been around for much longer than was previously believed, and that, at the time when we previously thought of humans as being strictly hunter/gatherers, some of them were actually living in communities and cities, and may have had knowledge of such things as agriculture, irrigation and sewage systems, and even technology. If you doubt this is happening, I suggest you do a little research on the archaeological research being done at Gobekli Tepe, in Turkey, and see how this one site has changed the human timeline.

But the aliens claim that Gobekli Tepe, along with dozens, perhaps hundreds, of other historical sites, are red herrings, placed into the game merely to confuse us. They mention Machu Picchu, Easter Island, Stonehenge, The Sphinx and the Great Pyramids, along with many other impossible-to-figure-out monuments of the past, as being here only to cause confusion and make it difficult to recognize that we're playing a game. The aliens also maintain that such things as Bigfoot and the Loch Ness Monster are also red herrings and, although people actually *do* see them, they don't actually exist.

One of the more interesting assertions made by the aliens is that the game can be halted for any amount of time – from a few seconds to thousands of years – and then restarted, and no one playing the game (meaning *us*) will notice. You could be walking across your living room, one foot in the air, when the game stops, and you'll just freeze in that position. Then, five minutes or thousands of years later, when the game resumes, that foot in the air will come down and you'll resume your walk, never noticing the game had stopped and is now slightly, or perhaps even significantly, different.

The reason you won't notice the change is that, along with the modifications to the game, a change has also been made to your consciousness. So, for example, if you wake up tomorrow morning and small, green, fire-breathing dragons with long red hair are mowing your lawn, you won't find that unusual at all because, after all, they've been doing that every week for the past nine years. Or so it will seem.

So far, I haven't mentioned the players of the game. In other words, us. Humans. The people of this planet. And this is, to me, the most upsetting piece of information to come out of this endeavor. I believe this is the *BIG SECRET* – the real reason governments around the world continue to deny the existence of UFOs, recovered flying saucers, and captured aliens.

You may have heard this before, put forth as a theory. Governments (ours and others) have been dealing with UFOs and aliens for many years, but have kept the information they've acquired secret because they believe ordinary citizens wouldn't be able to handle it – that some of the knowledge obtained from our contact with the little grays would cause us to freak out, bringing about mass suicides and the collapse of civilizations around the globe.

I don't believe this will happen. If I did, I wouldn't be writing this book. But both Teresa and I have been exposed to this knowledge and we have, so far, at least, managed to refrain from killing ourselves. The chances seem pretty good that others will be able to handle the bad news, as well.

And what, exactly is this 'bad news?' Well, according to dead Jimmy's interpretation of what the aliens told him, *all* (that's, like, 100%) of the inhabitants of this planet are avatars, or synths, or any other word you might use to describe a game player. That's right – the aliens claim that of the more than eight billion people inhabiting this planet, all of us are merely ... game pieces.

So, we're not real? Is that what this means? But avatars are representations of real people, those who are playing the game. So that means we must also exist somewhere *outside* the game, right? Like in heaven or in another dimension?

Unfortunately, no. That hypothesis – that in order to be part of the game we must also exist elsewhere – holds true for some players but not for others. The aliens claim there are two kinds of avatars playing this game, those that represent 'real players' and those that do not. This second group is referred to as 'ancillaries.' And both types are identical in all respects – you can't tell a real-player avatar from an ancillary. If you wanted to phrase this in a religious context, I guess you could say that some players of this game – some of *us* – have souls and some do not.

And this brings us to the scary part – that part of the story which apparently is the government's rationale for keeping this information secret. And, just a reminder, this is dead Jimmy's *interpretation* of this information. But, according to all three aliens, the number of real players in this game is minuscule. Little grays are not very good at such things as numbers and exact historical dates (which is why the start of this game is dated as 'around the time of Columbus'), but dead Jimmy estimates the amount of real players at somewhere between three and five *million*. That leaves more than eight *billion* of us in the 'ancillary' category.

And, unfortunately for the eight billion ancillaries, real players hold nearly all positions of power, in nearly all fields. Prime ministers, presidents, senators and other high-ranking politicians in just about every country are real players. So are movie and TV stars, famous singers, musicians, and other well-known entertainers, sports stars, CEOs of large corporations and other notable figures in the financial field. The list of fields is extensive and I won't name them all here, but I'm sure you get the idea. And while it is possible for ancillaries to rise to a position of power or prominence, it happens only rarely.

Do these real players know they're real and others aren't? The aliens say they don't but many of them suspect there's something different about themselves, that they're not like *ordinary* people. It's also possible that some ancillaries may come to suspect this difference as they struggle through life while others around them enjoy great success. But, just as with real players, it all comes down to a *suspicion*. Neither group – real players or ancillaries – knows anything about this with certainty.

So, chances are higher than 99.999% that Teresa, myself, and everyone we know, plus you and your family, and everyone you know, are ancillaries. We're all just game pieces, not real people at all and not even representing real people from some other dimension. And what does that mean, exactly? Well, for one thing, it means you're not going to go to heaven when you die!

God, Religion, Death, and the Afterlife

Let's start with the big question – does God exist? (Or, depending on your belief system, do Gods exist?) The answer, according to the aliens, is yes. Good news, right? Maybe not. Because God is not a being – not a he or a she or even a thing – but a force, like gravity. Throughout dead Jimmy's three notebooks, whenever this subject comes up, the aliens define God as *the force that makes everything work* or *that which holds everything together.* And, as such, *God the force* is not a *personal* God. He (for want of a better pronoun) doesn't care about us because there is no *He*, just a force that doesn't even know about us. We're just a game, being played somewhere far away and of no importance whatsoever. This, by the way, is why prayer doesn't work. Nobody's listening.

So, if God's not in charge of this game we're playing, who is? Good question. The aliens claim not to know. When queried about who they report to, they reply with vague replies, such as, *To those who listen.* Not an especially satisfying answer, but it does lend credibility to the idea that the three aliens were telling dead Jimmy the truth. After all, if they had the answer to *everything*, that would be a little suspicious, wouldn't it? I'm pretty sure nobody, not even little gray aliens, knows everything.

Which brings us to religion. I'm sure lots of people will find this part offensive but, hey, I'm just telling you what was in the notebooks. Believe it or don't believe it – I don't care. But if you don't like the news I'm about to impart, please don't blame me. I'm just the messenger.

All religions are fake. That's the message. All three aliens insisted that no one playing this game possesses any inherent knowledge about the nature of God or about *anything* that happens outside the game. That includes preachers, psychics, those who claim they can communicate with the dead, and the like. No one knows for sure if Woofie, your dog when you were nine years old, is now up in heaven playing fetch with your great-grandfather, no matter what they tell you. And, by the way, it seems highly unlikely that would be the case because, according to the aliens, all animals fall into the *ancillary* category. They aren't real!

So what happens when you die? Is there a heaven, or some comparable place where good people go? Is there a reward for living a good life here in this game?

Unfortunately for all of us ancillaries, the answer is no. Heaven is not in our future. No matter how good a life we lead, ancillaries do not get promoted to real players. We're not real, and when we die, we cease to exist. End of story. Game over. We're just ... dead! As Teresa said when we first discovered this news, "That's kind of a bummer, man!"

But for real players, the story is different. When the avatar of a real player dies, the real player awakens on the *other side*. This other side supposedly is a heaven-like realm without poverty, crime, disease, or death, but it is based on science, not magic. No one there can snap their fingers and make a delicious lunch instantly appear, for example. But there are machines that can do it.

However, even though life on this other side is so idyllic, so nearly perfect, it can also be a little boring, a little monotonous. It can inspire thoughts such as, *I wish something – anything – exciting would happen.* And so games were developed – in this case, the Conflict Game, as dead Jimmy frequently referred to it.

The Conflict Game was designed to alleviate these bouts of boredom. In the game a real player can be a rock star, a professional athlete, a big-time gangster, or anything imaginable. We ancillaries are usually just the supporting cast, of about the same importance as trees or animals. Or so the aliens claim.

One other item I should mention concerns suicide. There is a penalty for real players who kill themselves as a way of exiting the game, according to the aliens, but all three of them claim not to know what that penalty is. Dead Jimmy, however, believes that the penalty likely is a temporary ban on playing the game, although he never explains what led him to this conclusion. Of course, there are no consequences for ancillaries. For us, everything ends when we exit the game. Once dead, we completely and permanently *cease to exist.*

The Little Grays

So, just who are these little gray aliens who claim to know so much about what's going on here in our reality? Where do they come from? How did they get here? And what is their purpose, here in our Conflict Game?

According to dead Jimmy's interpretation of what was shown to him, the little grays are biological androids – robots made of biological materials instead of being made the way we might do it here on Earth, using metal, wires, and computer chips. I've seen reports – reportedly from witnesses to UFO crashes and body recoveries – that claimed recovered alien bodies had no sex organs. That makes a lot of sense if Jimmy's interpretation was correct – androids don't really need sex organs. Their method of propagation is different. They're not conceived by means of sex and then born, they're manufactured.

But when the subject of who, exactly, does the manufacturing, comes up, the aliens resort to what is something of a stock reply throughout Jimmy's notebooks. They say they are made by the same entities they report to, *those who listen.* This type of vague reply is the answer to a lot of questions about their origins, where they come from, and their purpose, here in this game. Whether they just don't know or are deliberately being evasive is hard to tell, but over the course of the more than 20 years during which dead Jimmy interviewed aliens, he gained enough information to sort of *fill in the blanks.* (Much of the information about the aliens comes, not as the result of a direct answer to a question, but from Jimmy piecing together dozens and sometimes hundreds of small details, gleaned from multiple interviews over the years.)

For example, all three aliens claim that they come from right here, but what 'right here' actually means is open to discussion. At some places in the notebooks it seems to mean 'here on Earth,' but at other times Jimmy takes it to mean 'here in our solar system.' Either way, the aliens were not created on some distant planet and then brought here. All three suggested that they were created right here, inside this game, in a laboratory and that, perhaps, this laboratory was located on a large, *mother* ship.

The subject of the Pleiades, long rumored to be the location of the little grays' home world, comes up from time to time over the course of the 20+ years of interviews. But the aliens claim never to have been anywhere but here in our solar system and to not know anything about this so-called home world. According to them, their masters (*those who listen* and, presumably, those who run the game) exist in a separate dimension, outside the game, and the Pleiades do not really exist – they're just a projection.

The big question, in my mind, at least, has always concerned the little grays' reason(s) for existing here in our game. When queried about this, they claim to have two purposes in life – one is to serve their masters and the other is to act as *monitors* of the game. While exactly who their masters are is never really well defined (are they the ones running this game?) they describe their job here on Earth as protecting the integrity of the game – making sure we humans, both real players and ancillaries, do not destroy the game from within. They also say that, over the course of the past century or so, they have done just that – saved the game from destruction – on multiple occasions, and that all of these occasions involved either nuclear power or nuclear weapons. The nuclear accidents at Chernobyl and Three Mile Island are both mentioned as events that had the potential to destroy the game but, because of intervention by the monitors (other little grays, not necessarily the ones in captivity) that didn't happen. They do not, however, explain exactly what they did to prevent these events from ending the game, only that they did *something.*

The aliens also assert that they have the ability to control Earth's supply of electrical power. That somehow, just by pressing a button (or an equivalent action) they can render it useless. This power also extends to computers – they can shut them down or just assume control of any computer, no matter how fancy the encryption. They claim that, to prove to governments around the world that they have this power, they have taken over and then shut down the missile systems of several large countries, both before and after launch. They have completely deactivated the missile-launching capabilities of some countries – just switched them off – and they've also actually launched missiles and then made them useless, sometimes by blowing them up and other times by rerouting them straight up, out of our atmosphere. This last action, by the way, produces another unexplained mystery. What happens to the missiles after they leave our atmosphere?

Those Other Aliens

You're probably aware that some people believe there may be other alien species besides little grays. Reptilians and the Nordic type are just two of as many as a dozen different species with whom humans claim to have had encounters. That these other aliens have had interactions with humans may or may not be true but, according to dead Jimmy's aliens, they *do* exist. But, if this is a game involving little grays and avatars called humans, where do these other aliens fit in?

According to all three aliens, when humans see, or *think* they see, aliens of other species, there are two possible explanations. One is that the encounter is not real, just a *red herring* (defined as something meant to confuse us) and the other is that it is genuine but accidental. These contacts – between humans and these other alien races – are not supposed to occur, but occasionally they do.

So, assuming an encounter is real and not a red herring, who are these other aliens, where do they come from, and what are they doing here? Dead Jimmy says they're *tourists* – visitors from other games, just dropping by for a quick look-see. And these other games they come from are not like the games real-player humans can play – not like the game we're now playing or the games it is based upon. These other games are so dissimilar as to be nearly indescribable to humans.

When the subject of intelligent life existing on other planets comes up, Jimmy's aliens just laugh. All right – not really. Little grays don't laugh. In fact, they either have *no* emotional responses of any kind, or their emotions exist in a *very* limited manner. But, according to them, only our solar system exists as a real, solid entity. The rest of our universe is fake, just a projection, so places such as Alpha Centauri (our closest neighbor, 1.34 parsecs [4.37 light-years] from our sun and thought to be a possible source of intelligent alien life) and the Pleiades do not really exist. The planets thought to be orbiting stars in these systems are also not real, of course, and so there can be no inhabitants. As one of the aliens told Jimmy (with a chuckle, maybe?), *We are the only non-human intelligent beings playing this game – there are no little green men.*

So, apparently, as a real player, one can choose from a near-infinite number of games to play, and none of the others are anything like the game we're now playing. All of these games, however, are built around *conflict* and exist as a means of adding adventure and excitement to a near-perfect but otherwise boring existence (on the *other side*). And the game you, me, and everyone else is now playing is the one that involves humans as participants, little grays as monitors, and, of course, lots and lots of conflict.

Tidbits

Dead Jimmy's notebooks were full of facts, speculation, and questions about a myriad of subjects – way too many to include here (because of both time and space). But, while many of these are of little importance to our understanding of what's going on here in our game, there are a few I thought deserved at least a mention, if not a full discussion. I'll briefly mention them in this section and leave you to decide on their significance.

We actually are very small – not nearly as big as we think we are. In reality, our entire solar system and our projected universe would fit into the equivalent of a two-car garage. Or so says Dead Jimmy.

For a long time the science of physics has been searching for a theory that would explain the differences between classical physics (gravity, thermodynamics, atomic, etc.) and quantum physics. Sometimes these are referred to as 'big physics' and 'small physics.' The aliens say it's simple. Quantum physics is the 'real' physics, while classical physics is merely 'the rules of this game.'

Because little grays are telepathic, their communications produce no types of waves that humans can detect. They have no radios, TVs, cell phones, or other devices that send out signals we can perceive. So projects such as SETI (the Search for Extraterrestrial Intelligence) are wasting their time searching for radio waves emanating from different parts of our universe, because the universe we see is not real and also because the little grays that zip around our solar system (the only real aliens around full-time) have no need of devices that produce detectable waves.

Aliens think of us as *Players* and of Earth as *The Playground*. These terms, according to dead Jimmy, are the best translation of how they think of us.

All three of the aliens seemed to have an unusual interest in bridges. Over the course of the 20+ years of interviews, more than 37 different bridges are discussed. Many of these went unrecognized by Dead Jimmy (remember, pictures, not words, are the method of of communication) but he was able to identify some of them. Among those were the Golden Gate Bridge, the Sydney Harbor Bridge in Australia, the London Tower Bridge, the Coronado Bridge in San

Diego, California, the Millau Bridge in southern France, and the Akashi Kaikyo in Japan. However, Jimmy was never able to discover, for certain, *why* the aliens were interested in bridges. He theorizes they might be impressed by the many different construction methods used to create them, but both Teresa and myself find this explanation implausible. Throughout the years of interviews, the aliens never seemed impressed with *anything* humans do. And why would they be impressed? After all, they know it's just a game and, as such, nothing really matters.

Although all three of Jimmy's aliens seem remarkably similar – almost identical, in most respects – the last of the three to be interviewed claimed that it had tasted chocolate candy and found it to be most enjoyable. Jimmy seems to think this implies that little grays might have been constructed with a modicum of free will, or perhaps free will is an evolving trait, a side effect unforeseen by their creators (whoever they are).

If you can remember past lives, either while conscious or hypnotized, you are a real player. It's impossible for ancillaries to remember past lives because they've never had one. And they won't be having any future lives, either. Only real players can play the game more than once (actually, they can play it as many times as they like).

Humans have been trying for many years to reverse engineer items recovered from UFO (flying saucer) crashes. They have been successful in some cases – lasers, night vision technology (said to have been developed by studying the eyes of dead aliens), and, of course, the development of the digital revolution are some of the benefits of this reverse engineering. But the chief goal of these reverse engineering attempts has always been to produce flying machines (saucers) that have the same capabilities as the aliens' crafts, in particular speed, maneuverability, and anti-gravity. So far these attempts have been mostly unsuccessful, with the exception of partial success in developing anti-gravity. Jimmy's aliens claim humans will never be able to develop flying machines like they have, because controlling flying saucers is done telepathically, something humans cannot and never will be able to do.

As a side-note to this, the aliens maintain that all but a few of UFO crashes were not accidental – they were done deliberately in order to introduce new information and technology into the game. Apparently, if a little gray is ordered to fly its saucer into a mountainside in order to impart information to humans, it complies. As to who is doing the ordering, the aliens respond with typically vague answers (such as *those who listen*) that really tell us nothing. As for the few accidental crashes, the aliens blame those on lightning.

Some Final Thoughts

I think I've covered most of the important information developed by Jimmy throughout his years of interviewing aliens. Of course, each new piece of information brings with it new questions, and there's still much we have yet to discover and/or understand. Also, there's plenty the little grays *don't* know – they're not scientists, and while they claim to know many things (and evidently they do), they usually are unable to explain the mechanics, or workings, of these things, except in vague terms. For example, they say we're involved in a game, but they are unable to tell us who is running that game (*those who listen* is the best they can do) or where they exist (somewhere *outside*, perhaps in another dimension?). So, at the end, we're left with more questions than answers.

I'm sure the information uncovered by Dead Jimmy deserves further research, and I haven't even mentioned it all. In my hurry to get this book published, I have refrained from discussing interesting but, in my mind, less-important subjects covered in the notebooks. Among these were such topics as flying saucers, alien abductions, and cattle mutilations (they're using the cellular material to replicate themselves and replace "lost siblings," according to Jimmy). Obviously, the notebooks hold the opportunity for several more books on these subjects. Perhaps I'll even get around to writing one or more of those books. Or perhaps not – maybe it will be you. Why not?

PART III - UPDATES AND INCIDENTALS

In the past couple of months I've let a select few of my friends – other writers, mostly – read parts or all of this book. Some said I should go ahead and publish it, which I did. Obviously. You're reading it. Others advised me against publishing, arguing that it might get me and Teresa into trouble.

However, one of these friends put forth an interesting theory. He suggested that the attacks against us were designed not to discourage us but to make us curious, so that we'd *want* to investigate what Jimmy had to say. After all, most of what happened to us was minor in nature. With the exception of Teresa's ex-husband, Danny, no one got hurt. And we don't even know for sure if Danny's death was connected to this – it could have been just a burglary gone wrong.

And Teresa's garage blowing up could have been an accident, according to my friend's theory. They might simply have used too much explosive, and what was intended to be a minor event, maybe something that would start a small, easily-extinguished fire, became a large, garage-destroying mistake.

But the clincher of his theory – the part that convinced me he might actually be correct – was the fake alien seen by both Teresa and Bitsy. What was its purpose in all this? This was the one part of the puzzle that had never made sense. And if the fake alien was there to whet our curiosity, to remind us to keep at our task of decoding the notebooks, why did someone make it so difficult for us?

My friend's answer to this enigma was that he thought we had been dealing with *two* government agencies, each with a different agenda – one wanting to suppress the information in Jimmy's notebooks and the other wanting us to get it out there for people to see. According to my friend, only the government could do all this and get away with it. It had to be the FBI or the CIA or some other government agency. Maybe even one we've never heard of.

I have also heard from a couple of people who claim to possess personally-derived, clarifying information about some of the information in the notebooks. I'm not even sure what that means but it sounds intriguing. We'll see where it leads, if anywhere.

* * *

And now, a DISCLAIMER. This book is *science fiction*. (wink, wink)

* * *

Also, please don't contact me and tell me that *grays* should be spelled *greys*. I know you see it written like that, but the original description of these aliens (from where we get the name), given by claimed abductees Betty and Barney Hill in 1961, describes them as being gray in color. Since the Hills were Americans, and so am I, the correct spelling of this color is gray. Grey is the correct spelling in many other English-speaking nations, such as Great Britain.

* * *

It has been brought to my attention that one of the main characters of this story has the same name as me. This is just a coincidence. I came across the name (*my* name, Chet Novicki) one day and thought, *this would be a great name for my protagonist*, so I used it. But other than the fact we both have the same name, and I also studied Chinese Mandarin at the Army Language School many years ago, and I also live in Polk County, Florida, USA, and I also write science fiction, we are nothing alike. For example, I'm still married to my original wife and do not have a girlfriend named Teresa (my wife won't let me have a girlfriend, no matter what name she uses).

So, in addition to the fictional writer, Chet Novicki, who figures prominently in Part I of this book, there exists a real science fiction writer named Chet Novicki – me (an amazing coincidence, when you stop and think about it).

If you'd like to read some of my science fiction material, a sample of the first book in my *Podok Tales* series – a first-contact story featuring aliens with edible, incredibly-delicious tails – follows. It's an adventure story but, as you might infer from the subject matter, it's humorous in nature. Before you read on, though, how about doing me a favor and leaving a review of this book, *The Alien Interviews*? I'd *really* appreciate that.

Here's the sample of *The Trouble with Podoks*, book one of my *Podok Tales* series. You might have to look around to find the book, though, as it isn't available at all sellers.

The Trouble with Podoks (Sample)

Chapter 1

I should have known better. To go out walking, late at night, with a Podok, was to invite trouble. Actually, to go out walking late at night, even without a Podok, wasn't such a good idea in most large cities on Earth, and Honolulu was certainly no exception. Adding a Podok practically guaranteed something bad would happen.

He was having a drink in the Third Planet Lounge, just sitting there on his tail the way Podoks do, when I spotted him. I come here often, hoping to meet aliens, but this was hard to believe - a genuine, live Podok, less than 20 feet away. I immediately approached him.

Now, don't get me wrong. I'm not one of those alien lovers - not one of those humans who believes the answers to all of mankind's problems can be solved by our alien visitors. And I'm not in awe of them, either. Waikiki is full of aliens from all over this part of the galaxy. Has been for years.

In fact, what I am is a teacher. A college professor, actually. I teach classes in the cultures of alien races at the Pacific Institute of Technology, or the Pit, as most people call it. Because of my job, I've met and talked with aliens from all over, but never a Podok. Pode is just too far away for us to get many visitors. So when I saw this one, I had to say hello.

"*Ma kit po an, min Pode*," I said to him, and bowed slightly. May you live a thousand happy years, citizen of Pode. He had a vox-box taped to his neck and a plug over his ear hole, but I couldn't keep from showing off my knowledge of the traditional Podok greeting. It was a great way of introducing myself, I thought.

"You speak Podok?" he said. He bared his teeth and the dark, feathery rings around his eyes expanded. The result was an intensely fierce look, but, from everything I'd heard and read, Podoks were supposed to be extremely gentle. I took it to be an expression of surprise.

"Not at all," I said. "But I can exchange greetings in over 20 alien languages."

He bared his teeth again. Big, sharp, meat-rippers, they were. I decided he was smiling.

"I'm honored that Podok is among them," he said. "Won't you sit with me and have a drink?" The English coming out of his vox-box was clear and easy to understand. No doubt about it, the alien translators are much better than those made here on Earth. Smaller, too.

I pulled a chair up to his table and sat down. He was drinking one of those putrid green algae slushes all the aliens seem to like so much, so when the waitress came I ordered another for him and a beer for myself. All the while, I studied him out of the corner of one eye.

He certainly was the most unusual-looking alien I'd ever met. His skin was peach colored and his eyes, which were twice as large as a human's, were entirely red. A slender upper body, with short arms ending in two, seven-or-eight-inches-long, prehensile 'fingers,' sat atop a massive lower body consisting of two elephant-like legs and his huge tail. Covering all this were a T-shirt and jeans that included a matching denim tail cover.

His head was quite a bit larger than mine, and the top of it was covered with the same brown, feathery hair that circled his eyes, in a strip about three inches wide that ran from his forehead back over his head and down the back of his short, skinny neck. A Podok with a Mohawk, that's what he was.

"I've never met a Podok before," I said, "and I'm very happy to meet you." Try not to gush, I told myself. I have a tendency to do that when meeting an alien for the first time.

"My name is Roger Denton," I continued. I could see him fishing through his pockets for his business card, so I took out one of my own and laid it on the table. I've never met an alien yet who didn't have business cards.

He passed his card to me and picked up mine, studying it for a few seconds before putting it in his pocket. "Roger," he said. "A strong name. I like it."

I looked at his card. On it, in English, was his name - En-mek Steve - and nothing else. "Your name is Steve?" I said.

"A very masculine name, don't you think?" He bared those teeth again. Podok humor, perhaps?

"Very masculine," I agreed. I guess I shouldn't have been too surprised. I knew Podoks were major fans of Earth culture. They liked our sports. They liked our entertainment. They even had adopted some of our religions. It was all very strange, considering how far away from Earth they were. I suppose if they weren't so far away - halfway to the center of the galaxy - there'd be Podoks on every corner, sucking up Earth culture to take back to Pode. Still, using Earth names was ... well, unusual, to say the least.

He seemed to sense my surprise. "Many Podoks use Earth names now," he said. "They are much more colorful and interesting than our own."

I wondered if he was having some fun at the expense of my ignorance, but I decided to just accept him at his word. Despite the fact I am supposed to be an expert in alien cultures, I know very little about Pode and its inhabitants. The classes I teach are designed to prepare students to work in the visitor industry, and they concentrate on those alien cultures that send the most tourists to Earth. Since Podoks import Earth culture to Pode, rather than visiting, I've never had the chance to learn much about them, and I've never mentioned them in any of my classes.

Our drinks came. Steve's green stuff had pineapple, cherries, and a purple parasol decorating the top edge of the glass. Cute. I paid the waitress and told her to hit us again in 20 minutes. She smiled and nodded.

"My brother has a French name. Pierre," Steve went on. "And my sister's name is Setsuko. That's Japanese."

"Great," I said to Steve. Actually - if it was true - I wasn't so sure it was great, the way we're influencing their culture, but Steve seemed proud he and his siblings had Earth names, so I let it pass. Who wants an argumentative drinking companion?

"What brings you to Earth, Steve?" I asked.

"I'm here on business."

"It must be a very long trip."

"Very long," Steve agreed. "Almost four Earth weeks one way."

I let out a long, low whistle of appreciation. Four weeks! Most alien visitors to Earth measured their trips in hours, or, at most, days, leaping across space with less effort than it takes a frog to cross a highway, sometimes covering hundreds of light years in mere minutes. A jump here, a jump there, and - voila! Welcome to Earth. It was easy when you knew how to do it, and many of the aliens did. Four weeks was an incredibly long time to travel. No wonder we got so few visitors from Pode.

"Your business must be very important," I said.

"Yes. I come here every six months."

I did the math in my head. Four weeks, one way, times two round trips a year, equaled ... almost four months a year spent traveling between Pode and Earth. Incredible.

"And what do you do, Roger?"

"I'm a teacher. At the Pacific Institute of Technology, here in Honolulu."

"What do you teach?"

"I'm an Assistant Professor of Off-World Cultures."

"Most impressive."

I shook my head. "It sounds better than it really is. Basically, the kids in my classes are going to end up as workers in the tourist industry

- perhaps working at the spaceport or in some small shop. I teach them about alien customs, how to be polite - practical stuff, like that."

"Still, I am impressed," said Steve, sipping his drink.

"I'm on vacation now, though," I said.

"The people of Earth seem to be always on vacation."

I chuckled. "That's partially true - at least, here in Hawaii. The government limits the number of hours you can work in a year - it's called the Share-Work Program. Most people work only eight or nine months a year."

"And they are on vacation the rest of the time? It sounds wonderful."

"Except, you don't get paid while you're on vacation."

"Oh, I see."

"This way, everyone can have a job."

"And so now you are on vacation and someone else is teaching your classes?"

"That's right. I always have July, August and September - the third quarter - off, and I teach the other nine months."

"That doesn't sound so bad, even if you don't get paid," said Steve.

"I guess it's not," I agreed. The waitress brought us new drinks and took what was left of our old ones away. Steve and I raised our glasses in a silent toast.

"I am quite intrigued by your hair," Steve said.

"You mean the stripe?" I have a two-inch-wide strip of gray that runs through my brown hair from my forehead back, just to the right-center of my head, and I get quite a few comments about it. Lots of people are intrigued by it, and so, apparently, are Podoks.

"Yes. Is this something natural? Or is it a cosmetic enhancement?"

"It's natural. The stripe - my skunk stripe, I call it - first appeared about 10 years ago, when I was in my late twenties. I didn't like it when it happened, but since then I've gotten used to it. In fact, I think it looks kind of cool."

"Yes," said Steve. I like it, too."

For the next couple of hours we sat there drinking and talking, exchanging information about our respective cultures. Steve knew a lot more about Earth than I did about Pode - not too surprising, since he comes here twice a year and I've never been there. I mentally filed away everything he told me for future use. Perhaps I'd write a paper someday. Maybe even a book.

We'd put away six or eight rounds when Steve suggested he could use some fresh air. I looked at him closely. He did seem a little more blurry than he had earlier in the evening, so I agreed. "I'll walk you back to your hotel," I said.

I stood up. So did Steve. I wasn't prepared for how big he was - until now I'd never stood next to a Podok. He was huge. He towered over my six-foot-tall body by at least a foot.

"I'm staying here," he said. "At this hotel."

"Okay, then, let's take a walk around the block," I suggested.

And that's how we ended up walking along Ala Wai Boulevard, next to the canal, at one o'clock on a Wednesday morning.

Chapter 2

I knew we were in trouble the minute I noticed the three men following us. They weren't chasing us or anything. There was just something wrong with their ... attitudes. They were too nonchalant. Their voices were too loud. Their laughter sounded forced. They were too casual.

We were walking along the Ala Wai Promenade, next to the canal which forms the back side of Waikiki. Most of Waikiki is only three or four blocks deep, hemmed in by the ocean on one side and the Ala Wai Canal on the other, but there's a big difference between the front and the back. The front part is loud, garish, well-lighted, jammed with people, and safe. Back here, next to the Ala Wai, where we had foolishly chosen to stroll, it's quiet, dark, and dangerous.

I leaned toward Steve and whispered, "There are three men following us. I think they're planning to rob us."

"Really?" He started to turn his head.

"Don't look!" I said to him. I glanced across Ala Wai Boulevard and nodded in the direction of Steve's hotel, less than a block away. "Let's run for it," I said.

"Podoks can't run," he answered back.

"What?"

"At least, not as fast as they can walk." He pointed back, at his tail.

I could see his point. It was gigantic, easily a fourth of his body weight, and as he walked, it swung from side to side. Try strapping an 80-pound tail that swings back and forth to your butt and see how fast you can run!

"Can you swim?" I asked, taking a quick look at the dark, polluted water of the Ala Wai Canal, next to us.

"No. I do not know how," he replied.

Before I could come up with another suggestion, the men were upon us. They were a mixed lot - a Caucasian, an Oriental, and a large Polynesian who was nearly as tall as Steve. Here in Hawaii, by the way, an Oriental is a local person of obvious Asian ancestry. You have to come from Asia to be called an Asian.

Two of the men - the Oriental and the Polynesian - held electronic stunguns. They were pointed at Steve and me. I put my hands on my head.

"Put your hands down," said the Caucasian. He smiled disarmingly and said, in a very polite Australian - at least, I think it was Australian - accent, "There's no reason we can't go about this in a civilized manner."

I dropped my hands. "No reason at all," I agreed.

"That's good," said the Caucasian. He appeared to be the spokesman for the group.

I frequently have what I call inappropriate thoughts. These aren't about sex or anything like that - they're just strange thoughts that pop into my head and don't seem to fit with what's going on at the time. I was having one right now. As I stood there, about to be robbed, a brief thought about how nice it was to see cooperation among men of such different ethnic origins flitted through my head, then disappeared.

I glanced at Steve. His eyes were bigger and redder than I'd so far seen them. The dark, feathery circles around them were completely gone, having either contracted so much or expanded so much they could no longer be seen. He wasn't moving. Basically, he looked catatonic.

"He's a Podok," I said, hoping that would explain everything.

"Oh, we know. We know," said the Caucasian. He turned to Steve and held out both hands, palms down, then slowly turned them over, to the palms up position, to show they were empty. "Ma kit po an," he said.

For some reason, that really irritated me. He had a lot of nerve, knowing stuff like that. What right did a common criminal have to be spouting something obscure like a Podok greeting?

Steve appeared to be still in shock. Even though I knew it wasn't a good idea, I couldn't resist commenting. "Yeah, your hands are empty," I said. "But what about your friends?"

"Alas," he said. "It's a less-than-perfect world."

I had to agree with that. I started to remove my watch and ring.

"Forget that," said the Caucasian. "We don't want your jewelry."

I glanced at the other two men - their stunguns were now pointed at only me. I guess they figured Steve wasn't much of a threat. Ten feet away, on Ala Wai Boulevard, dozens of robocars whooshed by every minute, but expecting any of them to stop and help us was out of the question. If the occupants of those vehicles even bothered to glance our way, they probably thought we were just having a friendly discussion.

"Chipcard?" I said, although I doubted they wanted that, either. It was just about impossible to use another person's chipcard.

The Caucasian shook his head.

"What do you want, then?" I asked.

"Him," he said. He pointed at Steve. "We want the Podok."

My mind must still have been fuzzy from all the alcohol I'd consumed, or I would have made the connection right away. But I didn't. "Steve? You want Steve? What for?"

The Caucasian looked surprised. "Why, for his tail, of course," he said.

Suddenly, it all made sense. This wasn't a robbery, it was a kidnapping. And Steve was the intended victim. No wonder this street thug knew the Podok greeting! That made me feel a little bit better, but then I remembered I was witnessing a major felony, and witnesses are, from the criminals' point of view, both undesirable and frequently expendable. That made me feel a lot worse.

"What about me?" I asked.

The Caucasian shrugged. "We don't want you. You don't have a tail."

"So ...?"

He glanced toward the canal. "Jump," he said.

"What?" I knew what he meant - I was stalling. For what reason, I really didn't know.

"Jump into the canal."

"I can't swim," I lied.

He looked first to his left, where the Oriental stood, his stungun aimed at my heart. Then he looked to his right, at the Polynesian, whose stungun was also trained on my heart. Then he looked at me and smiled. "Two stunshots to the heart will kill most men," he said. "Your choice, mate. Jump or die."

I jumped.

The water was not particularly cold. I flailed around in it for a few seconds and then discovered I could touch the bottom. I stood up. The water was less than three feet deep.

Above me, the kidnappers were busily loading the still-rigid Steve into the side door of a white minivan. It seemed to me catatonia didn't offer much effectiveness as a defense, especially against kidnapping. Maybe things were different on Pode.

I waded awkwardly toward dry land. A cemented rock wall lined the edge of the canal. I clambered over the slippery stones and up onto the sidewalk just in time to see the white minivan disappear down the Ala Wai toward the Kapiolani business district. For a second I thought I saw Steve staring forlornly through the back window, but that was probably just my imagination.

Chapter 3

Standing by the side of Ala Wai Boulevard, dripping wet, trying to flag down a taxi, proved to be an exercise in frustration. And without my com, which now resided somewhere on the bottom of the canal, I was helpless. After dozens of empty robocabs passed me by in the space of about five minutes, I gave up and jogged the eight-or-so blocks to the Honolulu Police Waikiki Substation, ignoring the stares of tourists and the catcalls of locals along the way. Halfway there I started getting a blister on my left heel. I took off my shoes and left them on the sidewalk, socks inside. They were ruined, anyway. I arrived at the station wet, disheveled, barefooted, and out of breath.

The station was almost empty - a couple of hookers, a tourist filling out a lost wallet form, and two tired-looking uniformed officers. I approached the more-alert looking of the two with my story.

"Kidnapped, huh?" he said when I'd finished.

"Yes."

"An alien, you say?"

"Yes."

"An off-world alien?"

"Yes." A puddle was forming around my bare feet. I moved a step to the left.

"Wait here, please." He went into a room in the back and reappeared a few seconds later, beckoning me with his finger.

The officer inside the room - Sergeant Higa, according to a large, koa-wood sign on his desk - wore civilian clothes. He smiled when he saw me. "I'd ask you to sit," he said, "but under the conditions ..."

"Don't worry about it," I said. "I understand." I was doing enough damage to the station's floors - no need to ruin a chair, as well.

"Tell me what happened," he said.

I told him my story.

"I don't know much about Podoks," Sergeant Higa said when I'd finished. "Actually, I don't know anything about Podoks."

I nodded. "Not many people do." I was about to tell him I was something of an expert on Podoks, but before I could do so, he consulted his computer.

"Give me a short rap on the planet Pode," he said to the computer.

The computer responded in a pleasant-sounding feminine voice: *The planet Pode is one of two inhabited planets in the Pelsentra star system. It orbits its G-5 star once every 307 Earth-days, and, in many respects -*

"Wait," said Sergeant Higa. "Just tell me about the inhabitants. And make it brief."

Of the planet's four continents, two are inhabited by the planet's one race, Podoks. Podoks are kind, friendly, loyal, curious, and very intelligent. They have both a spoken and a written language, also called Podok. They attend school, believe in God, build cities, marry, bury their dead - in short, they do the same things as do other sentient beings throughout the galaxy. They are especially appreciative of Earth cultures. They also have large, fatty tails that are delicious when cooked.

"Large, fatty tails? Delicious when cooked?" Sergeant Higa laughed out loud. "I'm sorry," he said to me, still grinning. "I know it's not funny."

"It's not," I agreed. The carpet darkened around my feet. I decided to stay put and just ruin one spot.

"So they kidnapped him for his tail?" Sergeant Higa said.

I wasn't sure if he was talking to me or just thinking out loud, but I answered, anyway. "That's right. For his tail."

"Seems like a lot of trouble for a few steaks."

Finally. A chance to strut my stuff. I may not know all that much about Pode and Podoks, but I do know about their tails. "Podok meat is illegal on Earth," I said. "You can only get it on the black market. And it's expensive."

"How expensive?"

I shrugged. "Depends. Six hundred, eight hundred credits a pound, from what I've heard. You know the black market."

"Yes. Supply and demand."

"Anyway, it's supposed to be the most expensive food item in the galaxy."

"I can believe that. How much would you say it weighed? Your friend Steve's tail, I mean."

"About 75 or 80 pounds would be my guess," I said. "It was big. And thick. Especially at the base."

"So, 80 times 800 credits. His tail could be worth as much as ... 64,000 credits?" The look on Sergeant Higa's face was one of total disbelief.

"I guess it could," I said. I'd never actually thought of it in those terms before - price per pound and all that - and I was almost as surprised as Sergeant Higa to hear what Steve's tail was worth. Sixty-four thousand credits was a very nice sum. No wonder the kidnappers hadn't been interested in my watch and ring.

"Things do not look good for your friend, Steve," said Sergeant Higa.

"No, they don't, do they?"

"I suspect we'll find his body, dumped somewhere, in a day or two. Minus his tail, of course."

"I'm not so sure about that," I said.

The sergeant arched his eyebrows. "You don't think they'll cut off his tail?"

"They probably will. But I don't think that'll kill him."

Sergeant Higa leaned back in his chair and stuck a toothpick in his mouth. "So why not?" he asked.

"Podoks have been having their tails cut off for hundreds of years – maybe thousands," I said. "It doesn't seem to harm them. They even do it to themselves."

"They eat their own tails?!!"

"They don't eat them, they sell them. They're worth a fortune, as you figured out."

"This is starting to gross me out," said Sergeant Higa. "They sell body parts for use as food?"

"It's not as bad as it sounds. Their tails regenerate."

"They grow back?"

I nodded. "Quickly, too. Podoks who sell their tails - not all of them do, of course - can do it twice a year."

"Well, I'll issue a BOLO and a bulletin, but I'm not as optimistic as you seem to be about finding him alive."

"I appreciate your help - whatever you can do," I said.

Sergeant Higa tossed his toothpick into the wastebasket next to his desk and shook his head. "Life just gets stranger and stranger," he said with a sigh.

I couldn't argue with that.

Chapter 4

It was almost three A.M. by the time I got back to my apartment in Kapahulu, about a mile from Waikiki. I was tired, my feet were sore, and I smelled bad. I peeled off my clothes, which were nearly dry by this time, and threw them in a pile in the middle of the living room. Just one of the advantages of living alone.

A quick shower and shampoo later, I was ready for bed. I slid beneath the cool sheets and just lay there in the dark, trying to relax. It had been a nerve-wracking evening.

Poor Steve. I hoped he was all right. Even though what had happened wasn't really my fault, I felt guilty, anyway. I should have done something, although, try as hard as I could, I couldn't think up any heroic plan that would have saved Steve from his kidnappers and me from the polluted waters of the Ala Wai.

Be reasonable, I told myself. You did what any unarmed, out-of-shape, 160-pound college professor would have done if confronted by three stungun-wielding hoodlums. To do anything else would have been foolish. Still, I was mad about being made to jump into the Ala Wai. They didn't have to do that.

I'd promised Sergeant Higa I'd go to the main police station in the morning to look at mug shots. Be prepared to spend several hours, he'd said. More great news.

It was almost 3:30. I ordered a wake-up call for 9 A.M., pounded my pillow into a comfortable shape and drifted off to sleep, thinking about Steve.

A dream set upon me almost immediately. In it, I was back on Ala Wai Boulevard, with Steve. The kidnappers were there, too, as well as some other people whose features I couldn't quite make out. Steve did not have a tail.

"We want the Podok," the Caucasian was saying.

"Why?" I asked.

"Why, for his tail, of course."

I was about to point out that Steve did not have a tail when one of the featureless peripheral players stepped forward. It was my ex-wife, Linda.

"Why don't you do something, Roger?" she said in that whiny voice I hate so much.

I blinked back at her, not knowing what to say. What was she, a moron? Couldn't she see these guys had stunguns?

"You're a wimp," she said. "A great big wimp."

"Tell her to shut up," said the Caucasian.

"That never works," I said.

"Wimp, wimp, wimp," said Linda. She always did have a creative vocabulary.

"Tell her to shut up or I'll blow your ears off!" said the Caucasian. He pointed a huge stungun at my head. It was easily three times bigger than the biggest I'd ever seen, and it seemed to be permanently attached to his arm. "Tell her!" he said again.

"Shut up, Linda," I said. It was difficult to get much conviction into my voice, even though my life - or, at least, my ears - depended on it. I knew she wouldn't be quiet.

"You'd like that, wouldn't you? I'll bet you'd like to shut me up forever!"

I was about to agree with her last statement, but before I could get my mouth open, the Caucasian fired at my right ear. The stunshot came tumbling toward my head in super-slow motion, all reds and yellows. I could see it coming, and tried to get out of the way, but my feet wouldn't move. I looked down. My shoes were gone and my feet were glued to the sidewalk. The three hoodlums laughed merrily at my predicament.

The stunshot came closer and closer and then hit me in the ear. I braced myself for the expected pain, but there was none. Instead, there was a soft, intermittent ringing inside my ear, which grew gradually louder. Ring. Ring. Ring.

I opened my eyes. I was in my apartment, in my own bed, and my wall was ringing. "Answer," I mumbled, and then said, "Hello."

The sound of heavy breathing greeted me. Great! Just what I need at 3:45 A.M. - an obscene call. I was about to disconnect when a voice said, "Hello? Hello? Is this Roger?"

I sat up, wide awake. It sounded like Steve. "Screen, please. Not too bright," I said. The wall opposite my bed lit up, but it was blank.

"Roger?"

"Steve? Is that you?"

"It's me. Yes."

"Why can't I see you?"

"I'm calling from a com. A public com."

"Are you all right?"

"Yes. Yes, I am. I have managed to escape my tormentors."

"Where are you? I'll come pick you up," I said.

He gave me an address in Kakaako, a high-rise residential area halfway between Waikiki and downtown Honolulu.

"Stay right there," I told him. "I'll pick you up in 10, maybe 15 minutes."

"Roger?"

"What?"

"Please hurry."

"I'll be there right away. You stay out of sight until you see my car. It's a light-blue Elektrin convertible."

"Convertible?"

I guess a vox-box can't know everything. "No top," I explained. I gave him my license number and said goodbye. In less than three minutes I was dressed, out the door, and heading for Kakaako.

Chapter 5

It took me 10 minutes to get there. I turned right off Ala Moana Boulevard onto Ward Avenue, then left onto Queen Street, heading toward downtown. It had been a few years since I'd been in this area, but everything looked pretty much the same as I remembered.

Steve was right where he said he'd be - hiding behind some trash bins in the 700 block of Queen Street. I cruised slowly by, at first not seeing him, and then just catching a glimpse of him as he emerged from the shadows.

"Roger?" he called. His voice was a stage whisper.

I switched from auto to manual, braked and reversed to where he was standing. He still had his tail. That was good news. "C'mon," I said, pushing open the passenger-side door.

Steve started to get in and then stopped.

"What?"

"My tail ..."

"What about it?"

"It's in the way. I can't sit down."

"Can't you push it to one side or something?"

"No. It's too thick."

The Elektrin is a small car - it seats two - and getting Steve into it was something of a problem, but eventually we found the only way he'd fit - kneeling on the seat, facing backward, his tail where a human's legs and feet would be.

"How did you get away?" I asked.

"I climbed down the outside of the building. From lanai to lanai, all the way from the seventh floor."

I guess the disbelief I felt showed on my face, because Steve continued, "Podoks can't swim. Podoks can't run. But Podoks *can* climb, if they have to. And I had to. The doctor they hired to remove my tail didn't show up, and they were talking about doing it themselves. With a machete."

I winced. "That sounds painful."

"They were just going to hack it off. If it's not done correctly, it won't grow back, you know. I had to escape."

I could see his point. The threat of losing a major portion of one's anatomy could turn anyone into a climber, even a Podok.

"One more thing," Steve said.

I put the car in gear and pulled away. It was still dark - the street was deserted. "What?"

"They know I'm gone. They're out looking for me. They went by twice while I was waiting for you."

As if on cue, a white minivan turned onto Queen Street about two blocks away and headed toward us. Just what we needed - more good news.

"It's them," said Steve.

We were traveling toward each other, they toward Ward Avenue and we in the direction of downtown.

"Duck down," I said. "Maybe they won't see you." Steve lowered his head and upper body as best he could, but I could see right away that we weren't going to fool the occupants of the van with this maneuver.

The van approached us. The driver - it was the Oriental - sat two or three feet higher than did Steve and I in the Elektrin. He looked down at us as we passed.

"It's him!" said someone in the van as it went by.

I floored the accelerator. In my rear-view mirror I saw the van slide to a turn-stop and then take off after us.

Steve looked up. "They're following us," he said. In the footwell of the passenger seat, his tail began vibrating noisily against the floorboard. Thump, thump, thump. Fear, I guess, is universal.

Flashes of red light appeared next to the Elektrin's windows - stunshots. They were shooting at us. And getting closer.

"These guys mean business," I said through clenched teeth, sounding like some video detective cliche. I couldn't help it. This whole experience seemed completely unreal to me, like a dream, or a flik. This is not what a college professor usually does with his spare time. I felt like an actor, playing a part.

"Don't they know that Podok tail is no good unless it's removed while the Podok is still alive?" Steve said.

I glanced at him. Was he trying to be funny? I couldn't tell by looking at him, but his tail had stopped shaking. "I don't think they do," I answered.

Popping noises sounded behind us - once, twice, a pause, then two more.

"They have guns," said Steve. "Real guns."

As if to prove the veracity of Steve's statement, a bullet tore through my outside rear-view mirror, shattering the glass. I ducked, instinctively.

"They're catching up to us," said Steve.

"Hang on," I said. I cranked the steering wheel hard to the left and slid into a side street, accelerating away as fast as I could. In the past, this area had been zoned for light industry Dozens of narrow, twisting streets, some not even wide enough for two vehicles abreast, had been filled with automotive repair shops, laundries, and like businesses. The businesses were all gone now - long ago relocated to some less expensive area of the city - but most of the streets remained. I knew they were our only chance of getting away.

The Elektrin is a nice car, but it was made for low-speed city driving, not racing. On Queen Street, or any other long, straight street, for that matter, we didn't stand a chance of escaping from the superior speed of the minivan. But on these side streets, most only a block or two long, maybe we could lose them.

"Faster!" said Steve. "Faster!" His tail started thumping again.

I was going as fast as I could. After all, it's not like I do this for a living. An old cliche popped into my head - how come there's never a cop around when you need one?

"They're gaining on us!"

I slid around a right-hand corner, nearly losing the rear end in the process, and almost immediately had to turn left. Out of the corner of my eye I could see Steve hanging on tightly with both hands. The look on his face, I guessed, was one of desperation.

"Don't worry, Steve. I'll get us out of here." My voice sounded remarkably calm. I'm a natural at this, I thought.

Two bullets zinged by, a second apart. I turned again. The Elektrin cornered well, but it lacked acceleration. Each time I turned, a little distance would open up between us and the minivan. Each time I straightened out, the minivan would draw closer.

"Hurry!" said Steve, as a bullet slammed into the trunk.

Facing backward as he was, Steve had an excellent, although probably unwanted, view of his kidnappers' progress, or lack thereof. Each time I stretched the distance between us, he would visibly relax, sometimes with a loud, sighing sound, as if he'd been holding his breath. When the distance shrank, his tail would start vibrating and he'd become agitated. I guess a close-up view of hoodlums shooting at you is not all that conducive to inducing calm in a Podok.

A bullet whined by my left ear. I zigged. I zagged. I turned on every cross street that presented itself - first left, then right - taking each corner as fast as I dared. The white minivan followed. Finally, after what seemed like hours of racing up and down the dark, deserted streets, the van began to fall behind.

"I believe we may be outrunning them," Steve said.

I glanced behind me. It was true. The van was not as close as it had been.

"Thanks to your excellent driving," he said.

"More likely their cells are weakening," I replied modestly. And truthfully. I checked my own display. Still over 65% charged.

I screeched around a corner and we were back on Queen Street, headed toward downtown. "Hang on, Steve," I said. "I think I see a way out of this."

Ahead of us, to the right, a large delivery truck sat parked in a driveway, nose in. I turned the wheel hard and slid in beside it, killing the headlights as the Elektrin skidded to a stop on the left side of the truck. Steve and I ducked down, out of sight as much as possible, peering around our headrests. A couple of seconds later, the minivan sped by without seeing us.

"They missed us," said Steve.

"Great," I said. "Let's get out of here."

Light was just beginning to show in the eastern sky. Suddenly I felt very tired - the long night was catching up to me. I backed out and headed back down Queen Street toward Ward Avenue and Waikiki.

We hadn't gone a block when the cop I'd been wishing for earlier suddenly appeared from out of nowhere and pulled us over. Better late than never, I thought. Man, was I wrong!

Chapter 6

"PLACE YOUR HANDS ON TOP OF YOUR HEAD AND EXIT THE VEHICLE!" boomed a voice from the police car.

"Does he mean us?" Steve asked.

The amplified voice repeated the instructions, this time adding an emphatic, "NOW!!" at the end.

I leaned toward Steve, who looked as if he might become ill. "This is just a mistake," I said.

"GET AWAY FROM THE PODOK AND EXIT THE VEHICLE!" said the voice.

"All right! All right!" I yelled back at the police car. As I said, it had been a long night, and lack of sleep makes me irritable. So does being shot at and chased.

I opened my door and climbed out. "Don't worry, we'll get this straightened out," I started to say to Steve, but before I could finish, a uniformed officer grabbed me and slammed me up against the rear of the Elektrin, kicking my feet apart at the same time. I ended up spread-eagled on the trunk of my car, face down.

"You're in big trouble," said the officer.

I twisted my head around and looked at him. He was a burly, mean-looking fellow of cosmopolitan origin, with an extremely large stomach. His name tag identified him as Officer Johnson. "Was I speeding?" I asked.

"Shut up," he said, and kicked me in the side of the leg. I let out a yell and slid off the trunk, landing in a heap on the pavement.

"What did you do that for?" I said. I meant it to sound indignant, but it came out sounding whiny, instead.

"Shut up," the cop repeated, and kicked me again.

I looked to Steve for assistance. He was in his catatonic mode again. No help there.

"If you'd just let me explain," I said.

Kick, kick, kick.

I decided to shut up.

"Get up and assume the position," said the cop.

I did as I was told. Silently.

He patted me down, then cuffed my hands behind me and bundled me into the back of the police cruiser. His partner, a heavy-set, middle-aged woman whose name tag proclaimed her to be Sergeant Andrade, had been pointing a gun at me through all of this. Now she holstered her weapon and got into the driver's seat of the cruiser.

Officer Johnson got into my car. He glanced apprehensively at his alien passenger - Steve was still as stiff as a statue - then adjusted the seat, set the car for auto-op and pulled away slowly. Sergeant Andrade and I followed in the cruiser, she telling someone, by radio, that she and her partner had just apprehended the Podok kidnapper.

A wire grill separated me from Sergeant Andrade. The police had been forced to return to wire grills after lasergrids had caused several serious accidents to agitated arrestees. A couple of drunks had even lost their noses when they'd leaned forward to have friendly chats with the arresting officers. I put my face up against the grill and said, "I'm not the kidnapper. I saved him."

"Shut up," she replied in a bored, disinterested voice.

I decided to keep quiet. We could straighten all this out later, at the police station, after Steve regained his wits. I leaned back and tried not to think about how badly my leg was aching.

The first hints of Wednesday morning were showing off in the east. We turned left on Ward, went three short blocks and turned right onto Kapiolani Boulevard, heading east, toward the new police station in the Kaimuki section of Honolulu. At least it wouldn't take me long to get home after they released me. The new station - actually, they built it in 2104, six years ago - was only a couple of miles from my apartment.

It was starting to get light. A few cars passed us - the beginnings of what would become, in an hour or so, a monstrous traffic jam. Today, that thought didn't much bother me - I had a city-provided chauffeur.

This was all a big mistake. Nothing to worry about - it would all be straightened out eventually. I closed my eyes. Despite the fact I'd had only 15 minutes of sleep in the last 24 hours, I felt wide awake and full of energy. Adrenaline, no doubt.

We were stopped in the right-hand lane at the Pensacola Street light when it happened. A white minivan pulled slowly up alongside us. Suddenly, Sergeant Andrade slumped sideways and disappeared from my view.

I looked up just in time to see the minivan, which hadn't stopped, roll up next to my car, which was still in front of us. Officer Johnson turned to look at it, and as he did, someone inside the van stuck his arm out the window and shot him with a stungun. I winced. That was going to hurt like hell when he woke up. Despite my best efforts, I couldn't keep myself from thinking that it couldn't have happened to a more-deserving fellow.

I leaned forward and looked into the front seat. Sergeant Andrade lay face-up, eyes closed, a stupid grin on her fat face. I assumed she also had been shot with the stungun, and some pleasure area of her brain had been activated by the shot. Or maybe she was just dreaming. Whatever, she sure looked happy.

The light changed to green. Traffic moved around us with a minimum of complaint, assuming our little drama to be nothing more than a routine traffic stop, or perhaps a minor fender-bender. Only a small inconvenience. Better them than us, they were probably thinking.

The whole shooting incident had taken only a second or two. Now the van was stopped alongside my car, and two of the kidnappers - the Oriental and the Polynesian - were hurriedly loading Steve, once again, into the minivan. I couldn't see him, but I'd have been willing to bet that the driver was a certain Caucasian with an Australian accent. Or was that British?

My suspicion about the driver was confirmed almost immediately as the Caucasian appeared from around the driver's side of the minivan and opened the rear door of the police car. He leaned in and pointed his stungun at me.

I cringed against the rear door, awaiting the shot. I'd never been shot with a stungun, but I'd heard it wasn't all that pleasant, and I wasn't eager to find out if that were true. My earlier notions about me being cut out for this sort of thing were fast disappearing. In fact, they were completely gone.

"Well, hello," said the Caucasian. "What have we here?"

I peeked between my legs, which I had drawn up in front of me in an attempt to shield my head from the stungun. A stunshot to the body might knock you unconscious for 30 or 40 minutes, but one to the head would put you in dreamland for hours. Not only that, stunshots to the head sometimes caused permanent brain damage, and, on at least a few occasions, had caused death. "Hello, again," I said, trying to sound cheerful.

"Got yourself in a bit of trouble with the law, have you, mate?" he said, smiling at me as if we were old friends. His teeth were large and straight, but a bit on the yellow side for my taste. That's the first thing I always notice - a person's teeth. For some reason I've never been able to figure out, teeth are inordinately important to me. If you want to make a good impression on me, you have to have nice, straight, white teeth. What makes this little quirk even stranger is that my own teeth, while okay, are a long way from the perfection I demand in others.

"Just not my day, I guess." I smiled back at him, between my legs, as pleasantly as I could, considering my position.

"Obviously not. How was the swim?" He seemed to be quite relaxed and remarkably unhurried for someone who had just shot two police officers in order to re-kidnap their escaped captive.

"Oh, quite nice, actually. I've never been swimming in the Ala Wai at night before. Or in the day, either, for that matter." Of course not. Nobody would swim in the Ala Wai Canal. The slow-moving water of the canal had been polluted - badly polluted - for more than a century, despite the politicians' continuing promises to clean it up. Since it was out of the way - removed from the beaches and main walking malls and most of the tourists - government money never seemed to stretch far enough to fix it.

"I'm glad you enjoyed yourself," said the Caucasian.

"Well, thank you for your concern," I replied, trying to be as polite as possible. That's my advice when someone's pointing a stungun at you. Be polite.

"You know, you've made our task somewhat more difficult than we'd originally anticipated."

"Just trying to do my part for truth, justice, and the American way," I said, keeping the conversation light.

"Yes. I suppose so."

"And all's well that ends well, they say."

"Who says?" said the Caucasian.

"I don't know. It's an expression. You've got Steve again, so all's well that ends well."

"Yes, perhaps that's so, but ..."

Up in front, the other two kidnappers finished loading Steve into the side of the minivan. I knew my time was running short. "But what?" I said, hoping to keep the conversation going.

"It doesn't address the issue of revenge."

I should have kept my mouth shut. This was not the direction I'd wanted the conversation to take. "Revenge?" I said.

"Yes, revenge."

"Why should revenge be a factor?"

"You know. You do something bad to me, I have to do something bad to you. That's how it works."

The Oriental approached the police car. I heard him say, "We got him, boss. Let's go." The Caucasian turned his head and said something I couldn't hear.

Just for that instant, while his head was turned, I could see my opening. All I had to do was kick out, hard, knocking the Caucasian backwards into the door, which would hit the Oriental and knock him out of the picture. In the ensuing confusion, if I was fast enough, I could jump out of the car and start screaming for help. Or something.

I had just about finalized this plan when I realized I had missed, as they say, my window of opportunity. The Caucasian already had returned his attention to me, and once again the stungun was pointed at me in a vaguely threatening way. It was just as well, I suspected.

"Do you understand?" said the Caucasian. He didn't seem to be in a hurry. But then, the Oriental had called him, 'boss.' You can't hurry the boss.

"No, I don't understand," I said. "I didn't do anything bad to you. You started all this by kidnapping Steve."

"I suppose that's one way of looking at it. But I see it like this. Kidnapping your Podok friend is my job, and you made my job more difficult. You complicated my carefully-planned kidnapping, just by being there. That's the bad thing you did to me. My revenge was making you jump into the canal. That seemed fair to me, at least at the time."

"You threatened to kill me if I didn't jump," I reminded him.

"But, of course, I wouldn't have. That would have been way too drastic a revenge for such a minor transgression as yours."

I nodded my head in silent agreement.

"If you hadn't jumped, we would have thrown you in the water," said the Caucasian. "Not killed you."

I nodded again. It was good to know the man had a well-developed sense of justice. I felt a little less threatened. Still, he was something of an enigma - well-spoken, obviously intelligent and educated, but a criminal.

The horn in the minivan sounded - two short, tentative-sounding beeps. A look of minor annoyance flashed across the Caucasian's face, then vanished.

"And now you have complicated our plans once again," he continued. "This time, in a more serious manner."

"I'm sorry," I said. What could I say? From his point of view, at least, he was right.

"And so I am forced to take revenge."

"Please don't shoot me in the head," I blurted out.

"Shoot you in the head?" He sounded truly surprised - even hurt - by the suggestion, as though the idea had never even occurred to him. "I'm not going to shoot you at all, dear fellow."

For some reason, I didn't believe him. I maneuvered my legs in front of my face and braced myself, expecting the worst. Hadn't he said he was forced to take revenge? Some bad guys code of honor, I guess. Maybe, if I was lucky or if he was a poor shot, he'd just shoot me in the leg. Or the body. Anywhere but the head.

He didn't shoot me at all. Instead, he tossed the stungun onto the back seat, next to me, slammed the door shut and leaned down to the open driver's side front window. "Have fun explaining all this to the police," he said with a smile. Then he disappeared around the side of the white minivan.

When the light turned green, the minivan turned right, in front of my Elektrin, and zipped off down Pensacola. It seemed I was wrong about the cells - it appeared to have a full charge. I watched it until it went behind a large building, then sat back to consider the situation.

Steve would be all right - I felt pretty sure of that. He might lose his tail, but I doubted the kidnappers would seriously harm him. They seemed to be pretty decent sorts, actually. For kidnappers, that is.

Officer Johnson and Sergeant Andrade would probably be all right, too, once they woke up. I hoped losing Steve would reflect badly on Officer Johnson, but, deep inside, I knew it probably wouldn't turn out that way. Because they'd been shot while on duty, both Officer Johnson and Sergeant Andrade most likely would emerge from all this as heroes.

As for my own situation - well, I was going to have some explaining to do, no doubt about it. But I was sure the police would understand, once I told them what had happened and how I'd been set up. I felt confident that, after just a casual examination of the situation, any idiot would be able to see I couldn't have been involved in the stunshootings of two police officers and the re-kidnapping of Steve. I might even turn out to be a hero myself.

Wrong again.

Chapter 7

With the minivan gone, traffic resumed in the lane to our immediate left. In no time at all, I assumed, passing drivers would notice Officer Johnson, slouched unconscious in the front seat of my car, and notify the police. They might not be able to see into the police car well enough to see Sergeant Andrade, but they were bound to see Officer Johnson. The Elektrin was, after all, a convertible.

I made myself as comfortable as I could get with my hands cuffed behind me and settled back to wait for the police. Halfway down the next block, an overhead digital display told me both the time and the temperature - 7:03 A.M. and 81 degrees. It was a typical July day - by noon the temperature would probably be over 90.

In the front seat, the radio alternated blasts of static with short bursts of one-sided conversation that seemed to be composed mostly of numerical code. "That's an 815 at 994, 609. Right, 320." Like that. Sergeant Andrade slept through it all, smiling, while drool ran out the corner of her mouth and formed a big, wet spot on the seat. Very attractive - I wished I had my com. It would have made a great vid.

I looked up ahead, at my Elektrin. Officer Johnson was still out of sight, presumably unconscious. I wondered if he, too, was smiling. Maybe getting stunned wasn't as bad as I'd heard. How bad can something be if it makes you smile?

It occurred to me the Elektrin was the real cause of the predicament in which I now found myself. The cheap little townabout was totally unsuitable for this type of work - eluding kidnappers and such. Now, if I'd had a skimmer ...

Yeah, if only I had a skimmer. If I had a skimmer, instead of the Elektrin, I'd probably be home in bed right now, asleep. The chase by the kidnappers, getting stopped by the cops, Steve getting re-kidnapped - none of that would have happened. I'd have just goosed that baby up to 1500 feet or so and skimmed away. Steve would be safe in his hotel now, and I'd be at home, catching up on the sleep I'd missed.

Yeah, if only I had a skimmer. If only I had lots of things. Skimmers cost 10 times as much as cars, and I could just barely afford a car. Like many of the wonderful new devices modern technology had to offer, they were just too expensive for most people. Even the police still used cars for most work, and saved their skimmers for special occasions.

No, I'd never be able to afford a skimmer. I probably couldn't even afford the down payment on one. After I subtracted, from my meager pay, taxes, alimony to Linda, payments on my apartment and the Elektrin, a variety of insurance and other payments, and the cost of living in one of the more-expensive cities on Earth, I was doing well just to make it from one month to the next.

It was getting hot - 83 degrees, according to the digisplay. The front windows were open, but little breeze came through the grill into the enclosed back seat. One of the things that makes Hawaii a more-livable place than other tropical locations, like Mexico and the Caribbean, is that Hawaii is located in a trade-wind belt. The trade winds blow cool air over the mountains and down across the cities, cooling them and significantly lowering the humidity. The end result is that 90 degrees feels like 80.

But, of course, nature's air conditioning, as the trades are sometimes called, does not work well in the back seat of a police car with the windows closed and a wire grill blocking access to the front. Perspiration was beginning to drip from various parts of my body. It had been 25 minutes since the kidnappers left, and traffic had increased considerably. I wondered what was keeping the police.

I stared at the stungun on the seat beside me. It might as well have been a live, poisonous snake - I wasn't going to touch it. There was no way the police were going to find any piece of me on that stungun.

I wondered how Steve was doing - if he still had his tail. He really was quite unlucky to have been kidnapped by such persistent criminals.

Most kidnappers, I felt sure, would not have gone so far as to attack the police to get him back.

It was when a police skimmer flew over at 7:40 that I first noticed something was going on. The jet-black saucer skimmed noiselessly over the top of the cruiser, displaying a variety of weapons and lenses, all pointed down at me from small, round openings on the underside. I squirmed around on the seat in an attempt to show I was handcuffed.

Besides the skimmer, two other things alerted me that something was happening. The first was there was no longer any traffic. None on Kapiolani, in front or in back of us. None on Pensacola, either. Up ahead, a block in front of me, at Piikoi Street, two police cars, blue lights flashing, had blocked off Kapiolani Boulevard. It appeared this would not be a good day for morning commuters.

The second thing that alerted me was the police radio. It became much more active, and whoever was speaking was talking about me! I leaned forward, trying to hear what was being said.

"... squawk ... a situation at the corner of Pensacola and Kapiolani," said the voice on the radio.

There were a few seconds of silence.

"... It ... uh ... appears two officers are down, conditions unknown."

Another pause, presumably while someone on another frequency responded.

"The shooter has locked himself in the rear seat of a standard police cruiser."

What?!! The shooter? No, no - I wasn't the shooter!

The radio continued, "That's correct. He appears to be armed. The skimmer pics show a weapon on the back seat."

Pause.

"It appears to be a stungun."

Pause.

"We believe the hostage is the female officer - Sergeant Andrade. We haven't been able to get close enough to verify it in person."

Hostage? What hostage? I pushed my face into the wire grill and yelled, as loud as I could, "I surrender! I give up!" then leaned back and looked around. The only police in sight were the officers who had blocked off Kapiolani at Piikoi Street, several hundred yards away.

"We've got a hostage negotiator on the way. Be about five or ten minutes," said the radio.

Morons. There is no hostage.

"And the SWAT team. They should be there, already."

Great. I looked around again. Sure enough, the gray-suited, blue-helmeted members of the SWAT team were taking up positions around, but several hundred feet from, the police car in which I sat, almost completely helpless, despite what the voice on the radio thought.

"Sniper will take him out with one shot," said the radio.

What?!! Sniper?!! I slid down in the seat, so that my head was below window level. A sniper on the second or third floor of some nearby building would probably still be able to shoot me without much difficulty, but, somehow, I felt more secure with my head not exposed.

"They're sending out a robot," the voice on the radio said.

I peeked over the back seat, trying, without much success, to do so without making the top of my head an easy target for snipers. Less than 100 feet away, proceeding toward me at a very leisurely pace, was a small gray and black robot. I knew what it was right away - a communications robot, just like you see on the news or in flix.

I took a deep breath and tried to relax. They wouldn't be sending the robot out if they planned to shoot me, that's for sure. No, they wanted to talk, and that was good news for me. Once I had someone to talk to, I could explain what had happened and I'd be on my way to getting out of this mess.

After several tense minutes, the little robot arrived and stationed itself outside the driver's-side door of the police car. I could see it clearly through the wire grill. It was just sitting there, patient as only a robot can be. Calling them communications robots always seemed a bit pretentious to me. Basically, they were little more than police radios on wheels.

"Hello, hello," came a crackly voice from the robot. "Can you hear me?"

"Yes, I can hear you," I shouted back.

"Wait ... wait while I adjust this."

I waited.

"There. How's that?"

"Fine. Can you hear me?" I yelled.

"Yes. Yes, I can. No need to shout. Just talk in a normal voice."

"I give up," I said in as near normal a voice as I could muster.

"Just a little louder, please."

"I surrender!"

He - the voice from the robot - didn't seem to hear me. "My name is Officer Bob Sakakibara," he said. "I'm a trained hostage negotiator. My friends all call me Bob - probably because my last name is so long." He chuckled, then continued, with great sincerity, "I'd like you to call me Bob, too."

"Fine, *Bob*! I surrender!"

"Before we get to the negotiations, I'd like to talk about the hostages, Roger. It is Roger, isn't it?"

"There are no hostages!" I yelled.

"Well, all right, Roger. We can call them something else if you'd prefer. Do you have a term in mind?"

I sank back in the seat. Trained hostage negotiator, indeed. The guy - Officer Bob - was a moron. All I wanted to do was surrender and be done with this.

Officer Bob's voice came out of the robot, "Roger? Roger? Are you thinking?"

I ignored him.

"I have an idea," continued Officer Bob. "Why don't we just refer to them as the police officers?"

"Fine," I said. At this point, I really didn't care what he called them.

"Are they - the police officers - uh ... okay?"

"They've been shot with a stungun," I said.

"Uh-huh." There was a pause, then my new friend Bob said, "Listen, Roger, I have a problem."

"*You* have a problem? *I'm* the one with the problem."

"My captain doesn't want me to negotiate with you until you give us something ... as a show of good faith."

"How about, as a show of good faith, I surrender?"

Bob laughed heartily. "It's good to know you've still got your sense of humor," he said. Then, sounding more serious, he continued, "My captain would like you to let us remove the injured officer from the front vehicle."

"Go ahead, he's all yours. Take him," I said.

"You won't ... interfere?"

"No. Take him. Take them both."

"One thing at a time, one thing at a time," said Officer Bob. He had a very soothing voice. I wondered if that's why he ended up as a hostage negotiator.

"We're going to send two officers out to retrieve the injured officer," Bob said. "They'll be fully shielded, so it would be useless for you -"

"I'm not going to do anything!" I yelled.

"Good, good," Officer Bob said soothingly. "They're coming out now."

Two uniformed officers, completely surrounded by bullet-proof plastic shields, came cautiously forward to retrieve the inert Officer Johnson from my car. They crept to the side of the Elektrin, carefully opened the driver's door, and slid the still-unconscious Officer Johnson out onto a gurney. Then, without turning their backs on me, they retreated with their prize. I couldn't see whether or not Officer Johnson was smiling.

"See? That wasn't so difficult, was it?" said Bob. There was only one way to describe his voice. Soothing.

"I agree," I said. "So now I give up."

Bob chuckled. "My, my, you are an impatient one, aren't you? We haven't even heard your list of demands yet."

"Demands? I don't have any demands."

"You must have some demands."

"Why?"

"That's just the way these things work, Roger. You've given us something - Officer Johnson - and now we're prepared to give you something in return. You give us something. We give you something. Back and forth, until this ... situation is resolved." Soothing, soothing, soothing.

"So I have to have some demands?"

"Yes. At least one."

"All right. I do have one," I said.

"Good, good. Now we're getting somewhere."

I didn't entirely agree with that assessment of the situation, but I said, "I demand to surrender!"

Officer Bob laughed. "You're a funny man, Roger. But this is a serious situation. There won't be anything left to negotiate if you don't make at least one demand. And you know what that means."

I didn't, but I didn't like the way it sounded. "No. What?" I said.

"It means the SWAT team will take over and bring this situation to a final conclusion," said Bob. For some reason, his voice no longer seemed as soothing as it had earlier.

I really didn't like the way that sounded. "All right," I said. "I'll make a demand."

"Only one?" Bob seemed disappointed.

"Isn't one enough?"

"I suppose it is. But two or three would be better."

"All right. Two or three, then. Let me think a bit."

"They have to be reasonable, you know."

"Fine. Two or three reasonable demands."

"Now we're negotiating," Bob said. He sounded cheerful.

"Listen up, Bob. This is what I want. First, I want my car - that's the Elektrin convertible in front of us - to be towed away to a safe spot."

"No problem there, Roger, old buddy."

"Good. Then I want Sergeant Andrade removed from the front seat of this vehicle and taken to the hospital for treatment."

There was a long period of silence on Bob's end. Finally, he said, "Say that again, Roger."

I repeated my second demand.

"I don't know if we can do that," Bob said.

"Why not?"

"It's pretty complicated."

"I'm a reasonably intelligent person," I said. "Explain it to me."

"It's a procedural matter."

"Explain it!"

"Well, basically, it's like this. If we remove - if you allow us to remove - Sergeant Andrade from the vehicle, this will no longer be a hostage situation. And, since I am a hostage negotiator, procedure does not allow me to negotiate a non-hostage situation."

"Which means?"

"Which means we'd have to get a non-hostage negotiator in here to replace me, and he'd have to start the negotiations over."

I couldn't believe what I was hearing. "A non-hostage negotiator? Why would you be negotiating with someone who doesn't have a hostage?"

"Well, I'm not sure, really," Bob said with a little chuckle in his voice, as if he couldn't believe my stupidity. "That's not my area of expertise. I'm just a hostage negotiator."

"Listen," I said. "I'm desperate." This was the truth.

"It's a bad situation," Bob agreed.

"This is all a mistake. I didn't have anything to do with what happened to Officer Johnson and Sergeant Andrade. I was locked up here, in the back seat, with my hands cuffed behind my back, during the whole thing. Now I just want to resolve this stand-off so I can clear this up and prove my innocence."

"Sure," said Officer Bob.

"So here are my demands. One, get my car out of here. Two, get Sergeant Andrade out of here. And three, I want the door to this back seat opened. On the driver's side."

"Don't know if we can do that, Roger."

"Wait. In exchange, I'll throw out the gun. When you open the back door, I'll throw the stungun out on the street."

"Hang on a sec, Roger."

Several minutes of silence passed. I assumed Officer Bob was conferring with some higher-up, maybe the captain he'd mentioned. Finally, he returned.

"Roger?"

"What?"

"I just want to make sure I understand your demands. One, remove the car. Two, remove Sergeant Andrade. And three, open the back door."

"Yes."

"In exchange, you'll throw out the stungun?"

"That's right."

"How do we know you don't have other weapons?"

"I don't."

"But we don't know that."

At this point, frustration, lack of sleep, and a sense of panic all hit me at the same time. My eyes started getting watery. I took two deep breaths, choked everything back, and said, "After I throw out the stungun, you can pick it up. Then I will come out of the vehicle. If I've got another weapon, you can shoot me. I'll be helpless, in full view. If I don't have a weapon, you can arrest me."

"You are willing to exit the vehicle at this time?" said Officer Bob.

"After my demands have been met."

"Just a sec, Roger."

I waited, taking deep breaths and reminding myself this was all a mistake. There was no need to panic. We'd get this all straightened out and I'd go merrily on my way, with a hell of a story to tell my friends.

"Roger?"

"Still here," I said. Where else would I be?

"We agree to all your demands, but we have some demands of our own."

"What are they?"

"We want you to stay on the far side - the passenger side - of the vehicle while we retrieve Sergeant Andrade and open the door."

"Agreed," I said. Finally, it seemed as if we were making progress. And just in time, too - the heat inside the cruiser was becoming nearly unbearable.

"We want to retrieve Sergeant Andrade and open the door during the same trip."

"All right."

"After you throw the weapon out, we want an unlimited amount of time to pick it up."

"Unlimited? It's getting hot in here, Bob."

"It will only be a minute or so. But we don't want any of our officers to feel pressured, or hurried."

"Fine."

"After we've picked up the gun, I'll be back in touch."

"Good." I was starting to feel better. It appeared I was going to get out of this without getting shot.

"When you exit the vehicle," Bob continued, "do so with your back to us and your hands in the air."

"My hands are cuffed behind my back, Bob," I pointed out.

"Just another sec, Roger."

I waited.

"All right, Roger. When you exit the vehicle, do so with your back to us and your hands cuffed behind your back, in plain sight."

"Okay. Let's go."

"Wait. There's more."

"More demands?"

"Yes."

I sighed. I never knew police work was so ... demanding. "What else?"

"After you have exited the vehicle, you are to take 10 backward paces toward the center of the street, away from the vehicle."

"Okay. Got it."

"One more," said Bob. "You are then to kneel down in the street, at which time officers will move in and take you into custody."

"Not taking any chances, are you?"

"Can't be too careful," Bob said cheerfully. "You could be a desperate, dangerous person, for all we know."

"I'm not," I said. And that was the absolute truth.

* * *

And that's the end of this sample of *Podok Tales #1: The Trouble with Podoks*. Thanks for reading. Hope you enjoyed the book, *The Alien Interviews*. If you haven't done so already, please leave a review. I'd really appreciate it.

Chet (the real one)

9 798223 154259